"I am the Great Serafina," the woman said, gesturing toward the opening of the tent. "Would you like to have your fortunes read?"

"Okay!" Zoe agreed. Zoe didn't believe in fortune-telling, but she thought it might be fun.

She hurried to the chair and sat.

Serafina set the first card down.

"Hmmm," she said. A small smile crept onto the edge of her thin lips. "It appears that you will make a bad decision."

"Uh, okay." Zoe laughed nervously. What a weird thing for the woman to tell her!

"Zoe, be serious." Mia poked her in the back.

The woman placed another card down and shook her head slightly. A dark look crossed her face.

"It seems as though you may be in some danger."

POISON APPLE BOOKS

The Dead End by Mimi McCoy

This Totally Bites! by Ruth Ames

Miss Fortune by Brandi Dougherty

MiSS FORTUNE

by Brandi Dougherty

SCHOLASTIC INC.

New York Toronto London Auckland
Sydney Mexico City New Delhi Hong Kong

No part of this publication may be reproduced, stored in a retrieval system, or transmitted in any form or by any means, electronic, mechanical, photocopying, recording, or otherwise, without written permission of the publisher. For information regarding permission, write to Scholastic Inc., Attention: Permissions Department, 557 Broadway, New York, NY 10012.

ISBN 978-0-545-20266-4

12 11 10 9 8 7 6 5 4 3 2   10 11 12 13 14 15/0

Printed in the U.S.A.   40
First printing, August 2010

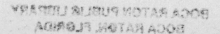

For Joe

CHAPTER ONE

Maybe this was a mistake.

It's too late. It's already happening.

Okay, this was totally *a mistake.*

Zoe Coulter could feel the quick thrum of her pulse in her throat. Her heart was beating faster than she'd ever felt. Her hands were clenched so tightly she could feel her fingernails digging into her palms. Her stomach sank into her shoes as the sense of foreboding grew. She stole a quick glance at Noah, still not believing he was right beside her.

And then she screamed wildly as the car of their roller coaster tottered on the edge of the highest peak of the ride for a few painful seconds before plunging toward the ground and then whipping them back into the air with a quick turn. Now Zoe couldn't help but laugh out loud as they spun one last time through the maze of metal before coming to an abrupt stop at the bottom. She *loved* scary carnival rides!

"That was awesome," Noah said as they stumbled down the ramp toward their waiting friends.

All Zoe could do was nod and smile. The roller-coaster ride hadn't been the first time that night she'd felt such an adrenaline rush. Her heart had begun to race the second she saw Noah walking toward her at the entrance to the carnival. Somehow, he had looked even cuter than usual in his dark jeans and the green T-shirt that matched his eyes.

Zoe stole a quick peek at Noah again now. The light Portland breeze had caught his dark brown hair and pushed it into his face. As Noah casually flipped his hair away with his hand, Zoe felt her heart flip as well.

"How was it?" Zoe's friend Tomo asked.

"Yeah, it looked *so* scary!" Makenna chimed in.

Tomo was standing next to Andrew and Zack, while Makenna stood slightly behind them whispering intensely with Zoe's best friend, Mia. Tomo and Makenna had known each other the longest out of the group. They had lived just a few houses apart

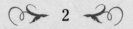

their whole lives and were still really close friends. Tomo had always been a bit of a tomboy and often preferred a game of football to a gossip session. Makenna, on the other hand, often preferred a good gossip session to anything else.

"It was good," Zoe said awkwardly, darting her hazel eyes toward the ground. She could feel Mia and Makenna studying her carefully. Ever since Zoe had met Noah at Tomo's house earlier that spring playing board games, she had thought he was really cute. And when Noah loaned Zoe fifty Monopoly dollars so she could get out of jail, Zoe had decided that he was more than just cute — he was one hundred percent crushworthy. Zoe's friends had all suspected that Noah had a crush on her, too, and they knew that tonight was the night they were going to find out.

"We were just talking about riding the Kamikaze next," Andrew jumped in, clueless to the girl drama going on around him.

"Yeah, let's go!" Tomo added.

Zoe smiled at Noah as they headed toward the ride. She was relieved that Andrew and Tomo had set the group in motion. She didn't want everyone standing around watching her every move with

Noah. Noah fell in step next to Zoe, and her stomach did another roller-coaster dive.

As they approached the line for the Kamikaze, Mia slowed her pace to a stop. Zoe instantly recognized the look in Mia's soft, dark brown eyes. She was scared to ride the Kamikaze. Zoe followed Mia's wide-eyed stare and looked up at the ride. Two massive metal arms each held a passenger cage precariously at one end. The arms swung in opposite directions like giant pendulums, building momentum and speed until they spun all the way around in a circle.

"Mia, this one isn't even that scary," Zoe said lightly as she put her arm around Mia's shoulder. "It looks *way* worse than it is. I promise."

Sometimes Zoe felt like she knew Mia better than Mia knew herself. After all, they had been best friends since fourth grade, when Zoe saved Mia from an overly competitive game of dodgeball. Mia was often hesitant to try new things, but as soon as she did, she was always eager to try them again. Like ballet, for example. It had been Zoe who had dragged Mia to her first class. But after five minutes in a tutu and those weird little slippers, Zoe knew ballet wasn't her thing. Mia, on the other hand, was totally hooked.

Mia was still eying the ride warily.

"It's like ballet, Mia," Zoe reminded her friend. "You just have to give it a chance."

"Can't I at least work up to the bigger rides?" Mia argued, pulling nervously on a piece of her long, black hair. Mia was Chinese with small, delicate features, and hair that was perfectly straight and super-dark. "I can't just jump on a roller coaster first thing like you can, Zoe."

Zoe sighed. She wanted Mia to have fun at the carnival, too.

"Okay, okay," Zoe agreed. "We'll work our way up to that one."

The friends headed to the carousel, then the bumper cars, and finally to the teacups before Zack convinced them to stop for some greasy carnival food.

Zoe devoured her corn dog as quickly as she could. She wanted to make sure they had time for all the rides. As soon as she was done with her last bit of meat on a stick, she jumped up from the table, crumbs flying everywhere.

"Okay, time for the Kamikaze!" she shouted.

"Zoe, we just ate!" Mia protested. She was still daintily picking at the last few bites of her sugar-coated, sticky funnel cake, but Zoe knew her friend was stalling.

"How about a few games first?" Noah suggested. He was always the quiet peacemaker among his friends. Zoe remembered the day they played board games at Tomo's. Noah brokered a deal to keep Zack in the game by setting up a complex loan system for him, and Zack had ended up winning!

"Okay." Zoe smiled at Noah. "But we *will* ride the Kamikaze tonight." Zoe winked at Mia, and Mia stuck out her tongue in response.

They wandered through the rows of games for a few minutes before Noah decided to try the ringtoss. Zack and Makenna joined in and lost out pretty quickly, but Noah was a whiz. Everyone cheered as he ringed bottle after bottle. By the end, he had his pick of every stuffed animal on the stand. Noah pointed to a bright purple stuffed bear and then handed the prize to Zoe.

"Here, it's for you," he said shyly.

"Thanks!" Zoe beamed. She was so excited she could hardly stand still. Zoe could see that Makenna

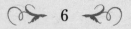

was having a hard time playing it cool as well — she wasn't usually one to keep quiet. Mia, on the other hand, just gave Zoe a subtle but excited thumbs-up when Noah wasn't looking. Zoe knew exactly what her friends were thinking — Noah totally had a crush on her!

After a few more games, a trip through the fun house, and a quick walk around the petting zoo, Zoe cleared her throat dramatically.

"Okay, guys, it's time." Zoe gave Mia a meaningful look.

"Time for what?" Andrew asked.

"The Kamikaze!" she shouted. Zoe noticed Mia's shoulders slump.

"Let's do it!" everyone else agreed.

Zoe walked over to Mia and put her arm around her shoulder again. "You can do it, Wang," she coached her friend. "It's going to be *so* fun, I promise. Don't be scared. Nothing bad will happen. There are straps everywhere holding you in. It's probably safer than getting in a car."

Mia sighed. "Fine," she agreed reluctantly. "Just hurry up before I change my mind."

Zoe hooted and grabbed Mia's hand, dragging her toward the monster ride.

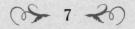

A few minutes later, the girls pushed their way through the ride's exit gate.

"Let's go again!" Mia cried. Zoe couldn't help but laugh.

"See!" Zoe gloated. "I knew you'd like it! It really *was* just like ballet."

Mia hung her head in mock shame. "I know, I know," she admitted. "You were right. I loved it! Now can we *please* ride again?"

Zoe laughed as she and Mia linked arms and dashed toward the entrance gate. Their friends quickly followed.

After two more turns on the Kamikaze, Noah asked Zoe to go on the Ferris wheel. At Mia's urging, the rest of the gang decided to go through the fun house one last time instead.

"I'm really glad you came," Zoe said as their car circled in the warm night air.

"Me too," Noah replied.

Zoe felt her face getting hot. She couldn't believe how nervous she was. She was usually so take-charge of every situation, but this was different. Her mouth felt like it was full of cotton balls. She didn't know what else to say, and even if she had, she wasn't sure she would be able to get the words out.

"So, Andrew told me you're a filmmaker," Noah said, breaking the silence. "I'd like to see some of your stuff."

Zoe smiled shyly. She willed herself to speak. "I wouldn't say filmmaker, exactly," she said softly. "But I do like making movies and stuff."

"He said you showed one of your movies in English class last year and Mrs. Wentz couldn't stop talking about how good it was."

"I guess . . . I don't know," Zoe mumbled, blushing.

"And you went to that film camp at the Portland Art Institute this summer, right?" Noah continued.

"Yeah." Zoe was secretly pleased that he knew so much about her hobby. He must have asked Andrew and Tomo a lot of questions!

It was true; Zoe loved film and making movies. She had played around with her dad's video camera for as long as she could remember, filming scenes around the house and driving her older brother, Conner, crazy. The summer before sixth grade, Zoe's dad had taken her to a one-day film seminar at the community college. After that, Zoe was hooked. Now she had her own video camera and had even made her first short film at film camp earlier that summer.

"Maybe I can have your number so we can hang out sometime." Noah's voice was barely audible. "You could show me your videos. You know, if you want to."

"Sure!" Zoe responded enthusiastically. "That would be cool."

Noah took out his cell phone and entered Zoe's number. Their car began to slow as they neared the bottom of the wheel. Zoe's heartbeat sped up. *Oh no!* she thought. *The ride's almost over and I've barely been able to say a thing!*

"Thanks for the stuffed animal," she managed to choke out as she patted the huge purple bear in her lap.

"You don't have to keep it or anything," Noah said with a shrug.

"No, I like it," Zoe answered quickly. She gave the bear an awkward hug, and Noah laughed nervously.

"Okay, good," Noah said. Then he touched Zoe's hand lightly just as their car jerked to a stop. The ride operator tipped the car forward and opened the latch. Zoe had to catch herself so she didn't fall out onto her face.

"Let's go, lovebirds," the man barked.

Zoe's face flushed again as she struggled out of the car. She looked up and realized that all of their friends were waiting for them.

"Hey, Noah," Zack shouted. "My brother's here."

"Well." Noah turned toward Zoe. "I'll call you, then."

"Okay," Zoe said, fearing her face might burst into flames at any moment.

Noah waved toward Makenna, Tomo, and Mia. "Bye!"

"Bye, Noah!" they called. As soon as the boys were out of earshot, the girls turned toward Zoe expectantly.

"Well?" Mia asked eagerly.

Zoe buried her face in her hands. "You guys, I can't believe how nervous I was!"

"I *knew* he had a crush on you!" Makenna squealed. "He's *so* cute! And I can't believe he won you that bear. That was totally adorable!"

"Tell us what happened," Mia said, pulling on the sleeve of Zoe's hoodie.

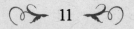

"He asked for my number and said he wants to hang out," Zoe said with a shrug. She was trying hard to play it cool.

"Zoe! That's perfect!" Tomo exclaimed.

"Totally perfect!" Makenna added. "You guys will make the cutest couple ever and — " Makenna was interrupted by her own blaring cell phone. "Shoot," she said as she glanced at her phone. "Tomo, we've gotta run. My mom's calling already. We'll def talk more about it soon, 'kay? Oooo, I'm so excited for you, Zoe! And promise you'll call me the minute anything else happens, okay?" Makenna talked in a steady stream.

"Of course," Zoe laughed.

"Okay, bye, Mia, bye, Zoe!"

"Bye!" Mia and Zoe said in unison, laughing as Tomo shook her head and waved a silent good-bye.

Zoe checked the time on her cell phone and gave Mia a sly smile. "Let's ride the Kamikaze one more time!" She wanted one more rush of excitement before the night was over.

"I don't know," Mia replied cautiously as she nibbled at the green polish on her fingernail. "Won't your dad be waiting?"

"Come on!" Zoe pleaded. "We totally have time. My dad won't be here for another fifteen minutes. *Pleeaase?*"

Mia laughed at Zoe's pleading expression. "All right, fine. Let's go."

CHAPTER TWO

The girls staggered off the Kamikaze, Zoe grinning wildly and Mia looking a little green, and headed in the direction of the parking lot to meet Zoe's dad. Zoe was surprised by how empty the fairgrounds seemed all of a sudden. She glanced at her phone. It wasn't even 9:30 yet, but it seemed much later. The moonless sky was so cloudy, Zoe could barely make out any stars.

The grounds looked darker somehow, too. It wasn't the bright and lively scene it had been just a few minutes before. A layer of smoke blew and curled across the dirt from a nearby hot-dog stand, casting shadows in front of the girls as they walked. Zoe shivered and zipped up her hoodie. She suddenly felt a little uneasy, but she couldn't figure out why.

As they neared the edge of the carnival, just before the gated exit to the parking lot, Zoe noticed a tent she hadn't seen when they'd come in earlier that night. Just as Zoe was about to point the tent out to Mia, a woman stepped out of the shadows. Zoe jumped back, startled.

"Good evening, girls," the woman said, though her heavy accent made the words sound more like "Good evunning, gulls." The woman had light olive skin and thick, dark eyebrows. She wore a black floor-length sheath dress and tattered leather sandals. A massive bun of black hair with a few streaks of gray was piled on top of her head.

"I am the Great Serafina," the woman said, gesturing toward the opening of the tent. "Would you like to have your fortunes read?"

Zoe and Mia exchanged glances and giggled nervously.

"Um, that's okay," Mia responded. "We have to go."

"I'll do them for free since the carnival is about to close for the night," the woman offered.

Zoe surveyed the woman's face closely. Her eyes

were a weird color — almost yellow and translucent, like you could see right through them. The hint of a smile danced on her thin, pursed lips, making her seem friendly despite her intense eyes. Still, there was something a little strange about her. But at the same time, she was offering to read their fortunes for free, so that seemed pretty nice.

"Um, okay," Zoe agreed. She didn't really believe in fortune-telling or magic, but she thought it might be fun. Plus, she was always looking for ideas for her next film, and she never knew where she might find them.

Mia checked her watch anxiously. "Zoe, what about your dad?"

"He'll wait," Zoe said. Once something was set in her mind, Zoe always had to follow through. "Come on, it will be funny!"

The Great Serafina bristled at Zoe's comment, but Zoe didn't notice. She just strode right into the tent. Mia hesitated, but then sighed and jogged over to duck inside behind Zoe.

The tent was small. There were burning candles everywhere, and the scent of them hung thick in the air. Zoe sneezed loudly. There was a warm, almost cozy feeling to the small space, but when Zoe studied her surroundings more closely, there was something kind of creepy about it, too. The single cot and the low stand holding a hot plate and a jug of water seemed normal enough, but the row of antique-looking bottles filled with strange liquids and plants seemed a little odd. Just as soon as she'd thought it, Zoe laughed to herself and brushed it off. *That stuff is all for show. There's no way any of this is real.*

A small folding table and two chairs were positioned in the center of the room. The table was covered with a black tablecloth and was bare except for a row of melting candles on one side.

Serafina held out a chair and motioned for Mia to sit down. Mia glanced apprehensively at Zoe before taking a seat. Zoe smiled and winked at Mia, which was what she always did when she knew Mia was nervous about something.

"Now, let's see what the cards can tell us, shall we?" said the woman, her face bathed in candlelight. She rested a pair of thick-rimmed glasses on her nose and shifted a deck of cards between her hands. The cards seemed to have appeared out of nowhere. Zoe stood directly over Serafina's right shoulder. She made a face at Mia and giggled.

"Maybe she'll tell you who you're gonna have for math next year, Mia." Zoe giggled again. She couldn't seem to stop laughing now — it all seemed so silly.

Serafina narrowed her catlike eyes over her glasses and stared back at Zoe for a long breath.

Mia watched the woman's expression. "Zoe, shhhhh."

"What?" Zoe asked innocently. "You don't like math. . . . It was a joke." Zoe wondered why Mia was taking this so seriously. The woman was obviously a fake. Everything about the tent seemed like it was set up as an act. *Well, everything except that weird snake head,* Zoe thought as she noticed a mounted snake head with outstretched jaws nestled on a piece of red satin in the corner of the tent. A small, ominous-looking bottle of liquid was propped between the snake's jaws. The snake didn't look fake. In fact, it looked pretty real. And creepy.

"Have you had your cards read before?" The woman ignored Zoe and focused on Mia.

"Um, no," Mia replied quietly.

"Well, I come from a long line of Italian fortune-tellers," said Serafina. "You will not be disappointed. Let's begin."

Serafina slowly laid a tarot card on the table with her long, bony fingers. After a minute of silence, she began.

"You will start a new journey soon," she said to Mia in a low voice.

"Yeah, seventh grade," Zoe mumbled under her breath. This time the woman turned all the way around in her chair and shot Zoe a glare. As soon as their eyes met, Zoe felt her insides turn to ice. The uneasy feeling she'd had outside the tent came flooding back. At first the woman had seemed nice and friendly enough, but when she glared at Zoe, there was something scary about her eyes. It was almost as though she was looking straight into Zoe and reading her thoughts. Zoe decided to stop joking around.

Serafina turned her attention back to Mia and placed another card on the table. "This journey, while not easy, will reap long-term happiness." She smiled warmly at Mia, and Zoe could see Mia relax a little in her chair.

Serafina tapped her bloodred fingernail on the next card she put down. "Your passion in life will serve you well."

Mia beamed. "I want to be a dancer!"

The woman returned Mia's smile and nodded. "And you shall."

At the end of the fortune, the woman handed Mia a small coin with a pyramid on it.

"This, dear, shall seal your fortune," she told Mia as she placed the coin in her palm and folded Mia's fingers over it. "Always carry it with you."

"Thanks!" Mia said brightly. "Looks like it's gonna be a good year. Your turn, Zoe!"

Serafina turned again in her chair and watched intently as Zoe made her way around the table to the other waiting chair. Zoe handed Mia her stuffed bear, hurried to the chair, and sat. She was excited to hear her fortune now that Mia's had been so fun.

The woman cleared her throat and set the first card down.

"Hmmm," she said as a small smile crept onto the edge of her thin lips. "It appears that you will make a bad decision."

"Uh, okay." Zoe laughed nervously.

"Zoe, be serious." Mia poked her in the back.

The woman placed another card down and shook her head slightly. "This decision may lead to some regrettable events."

"Hey!" Zoe interrupted. She wasn't feeling so excited anymore. "Mia's fortune was way better!"

Serafina took off her glasses and set them on the table. "Excuse me?" she said slowly.

"Zoe . . ." Mia started.

Zoe's pulse quickened a little as Serafina stared at her, but she continued, anyway. "Mia's was way better. How come mine is just bad stuff?"

"Do you think I'm just making this up?" The woman flicked her hand in the air and her voice rose with irritation.

"Well, I just . . ." Zoe stumbled. "Why can't mine be good, too?"

Serafina let a long slow breath escape from her lips. It sounded like the air leaking out of a bike tire, or a snake hissing. "Would you like me to finish or not?"

"I guess so," Zoe said, though she wasn't sure she really *did* want her to continue.

The woman quickly placed the next card on the table. This time a dark look crossed her face.

"It seems as though you may be in some danger."

"Oh no, Zoe!" Mia gasped.

Zoe shifted awkwardly in her chair. Now she

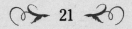

really wanted to get out of the tent, but she waited for Serafina to finish.

The woman sat perfectly still and continued to stare at the cards on the table. Zoe waited tensely for her to speak. After another minute of silence, Zoe cleared her throat. "Um, is that it?" she asked tentatively.

Serafina suddenly lifted her gaze and locked eyes with Zoe. Zoe's pulse sped as she waited for the woman to say something, but she just stared straight through Zoe with the same glassy expression.

"Zoe, I think we should go," Mia whispered nervously, hugging Zoe's bear to her chest.

Zoe nodded, her voice caught in her throat. Serafina's behavior wasn't making any sense, and Zoe was starting to think that the woman's act was more creepy than funny. Zoe moved to get up when suddenly Serafina stood and walked abruptly to Zoe's side of the table. She faced Zoe, her catlike eyes piercing right through her. Zoe stood up slowly and felt the space of the tent tighten around her. She felt dizzy. Why was the woman acting so weird?

"I must give you something to seal your fortune," Serafina finally said in a monotone voice, a creepy smile edging her lips again. She raised her hands and closed her fingers around the leather cord of the necklace she was wearing. She held the necklace out in front of her and moved to place it around Zoe's neck with a robotic motion. Zoe froze.

"What are you doing?" she asked, wide-eyed. A weird feeling came over Zoe. Her arms and legs felt heavy. She had no choice but to let Serafina put the necklace around her neck.

"I am bestowing the power of the snake eye on you," Serafina replied mechanically as she waved her left hand in front of the necklace. *"Il potere dell'occhio di serpente . . . Il potere dell'occhio di serpente . . . Il potere dell'occhio di serpente."*

All the color drained from Zoe's face. What was with the creepy chanting? Zoe wasn't sure, but she thought the woman might have been speaking Italian. She glanced at Mia. Her face was an ashy gray color. Mia looked terrified.

"I . . . I can't take this," Zoe said with a shake of her head. She reached up to remove the necklace, but Serafina's hand shot out to stop her.

"You have no choice," the woman said eerily. "The snake eye has chosen. It is yours."

"Zoe, we'd better go before your dad gets worried." Mia shifted nervously from one foot to the other. She had her hand on the opening of the tent and was already stepping outside.

Zoe could hear the tension in Mia's voice. "Yeah, okay." She backed away from the woman and took a wide step around her to get to the opening of the tent.

Once Zoe was outside, she took a deep breath. The air was surprisingly cold, but Zoe felt like she could finally breathe again. She looked down at the necklace. The tarnished silver pendant looked like a tightly coiled snake that had formed the shape of an eye. In the center of the eye sat a large red jewel. The necklace looked very old and seemed to weigh a hundred pounds. Zoe could feel the weight of it around her neck. The snake on the necklace was a little disturbing, but there was something about it that she liked. She touched the stone with her finger and felt her whole body grow warm.

She turned to look at the tent, wondering if she should try again to give the necklace back — even though for some weird reason she wanted to keep it. Serafina was standing in the opening with the flicker of candlelight around her. The shadows on the tent behind her looked like giant flames on the wall.

Suddenly, Serafina called out to Zoe. "Good luck," she said in the same deep, monotone voice. Then she threw her head back and laughed. The sound was evil and earsplitting.

A serious chill zinged down Zoe's spine. The candles made it look like the woman's eyes were glowing like firelight, too. Zoe turned and ran toward her dad's car. Mia was already waiting inside.

CHAPTER THREE

Mia returned to Zoe's bedroom after brushing her teeth. "So I want to hear more about . . . Zoe . . . Zoe?"

Zoe jumped out of the closet next to the bedroom door. "BOO!"

"Baaaahhhh!" Mia stumbled backward, clutching her toothbrush to her chest.

Zoe fell onto the bed, laughing.

"Zoe, you totally scared me half to death!"

"Sorry, I couldn't resist."

Zoe's window creaked, making her jump this time. The old Victorian house she'd lived in her entire life seemed to make more noise each year. The floorboards groaned and the windows creaked constantly. She walked over to her bedroom window and looked outside. There were strange patches of mist dotting the grass and street below, and an odd chill was in the air. Nights in Portland in the middle of August were usually much warmer. Zoe shuddered. She quickly drew the window closed, locked it, and pulled the curtains tightly together. After the whole fortune-telling incident, she felt a little more on edge than she cared to admit. Zoe was hardly ever scared, and she was determined to prove to herself that her uneasy feeling was just a figment of her own imagination.

Zoe ran back to her bed and tucked her feet under the comforter. She arranged a stack of pillows in the middle of the bed, took a flashlight out of her nightstand, and clicked off the lamp next to her. "Come on, let's tell ghost stories!"

Zoe and Mia spent at least two nights a week at each other's houses in the summertime and telling scary stories was part of their sleepover ritual. Plus, Zoe wanted to distract herself from thinking about the woman from the carnival.

"I'm already scared enough, thanks," Mia said. "Between your creepy fortune and you jumping out at me, I'm done!"

"Yeah, that was pretty weird," Zoe admitted. "I

think Serafina made my fortune creepy on purpose because she got annoyed by my jokes." Zoe wanted to put the woman out of her mind, but it was hard to do with the heavy pendant hanging around her neck as a constant reminder. She had thought about taking it off as soon as they got home, but for some reason she couldn't explain or understand, she had decided to keep it on. Zoe wasn't much of a jewelry person, unless it was a leather cuff bracelet or a funky plastic ring. She didn't even have her ears pierced. But there was something about the necklace that made removing it seem wrong somehow. She was too weirded out by the whole thing to tell Mia. The best thing she could think to do was to remind herself that spells and trances and ghosts were all . . . well, stories — as in *fiction*.

"So . . . ghost stories?" Zoe urged again.

Mia traced the red abstract flower pattern on Zoe's comforter with her finger. "Okay, fine," she finally agreed with a halfhearted sigh. "You go first."

Zoe grinned and turned the flashlight beam on her chin, illuminating the freckles dotting her cheeks and making her face look distorted in the shadows.

"Okay. One night a young couple was driving home from the movies. It was pitch-black outside —

there wasn't even any moonlight in the sky. Just as they got to an old country road, their car broke down."

"Oh, good one," Mia said approvingly.

"The man decided he would walk back toward the main road to a house they had seen and ask for help. He thought the woman should stay in the car. If anyone drove by, she could flag them down."

"Oh, it's never a good idea to split up!" Mia exclaimed with a shake of her head.

"So the man kissed the woman and set off for the house," Zoe continued. "The woman sat in the car in the dark and waited. She turned the dial on the stereo, hoping to get a radio station, but it was all static . . . until a voice came through the radio and said, 'Beware! Beware!' Just then, the woman turned and looked out the window. There was a . . ."

Suddenly, there was a loud scratching sound against Zoe's bedroom window.

"AHHHHH!" Mia and Zoe screamed in unison.

"Did you hear that?" Mia asked, her voice shaking.

"Yes! Why else would I have screamed?" Zoe whispered. "What was it?"

They heard the scratching again.

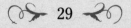

Mia gripped Zoe's arm. "Go look."

Zoe gripped back, her heart racing. The image of Serafina's translucent eyes popped into her head. "YOU go look."

Zoe clicked on the bedside lamp, and the girls sat rigid on the bed listening for another sound. And then it came.

Zoe held her breath, shot up from the bed, ran to the window, and flung back the curtain. Both girls screamed again. Then Zoe laughed.

"It's just a tree branch," she said.

Mia fell back on Zoe's bed and laughed with relief.

"I see Wendell on the lawn, though," Zoe said. "I'm going to go let him in."

Zoe walked slowly down the stairs to the front door to let her giant brown tabby cat, Wendell, inside. She took deep breaths, trying to calm herself. She hated to admit how scared she had been. *Of course it was just a tree branch,* she told herself. *There's no such thing as ghosts, right?* But as Zoe opened the front door and watched Wendell scoot past her and into the kitchen, she couldn't help but notice that the air was completely still — cold and still. What could have moved the tree branch against the window if there was no wind?

Zoe shuddered again and locked and bolted the door before running back upstairs to her room. Mia was already snuggled up in Zoe's summer camp sleeping bag, looking sleepy and content. Mia was usually the one who got really freaked out by creaky noises in the night, especially in Zoe's old house, while Zoe had always thought of herself as the more reasonable one. But tonight Zoe felt like a real scaredy-cat.

Zoe got in bed and reached over to turn off the lamp when she remembered the necklace. She looked down at the red stone and the ugly coiled snake and shook her head. *I shouldn't be wearing this thing anymore,* she thought. She sat up in bed and moved to take the necklace off, but something stopped her hands. It was like an invisible force surrounded the necklace and made it impossible for Zoe to remove it. Zoe felt clammy and light-headed. She looked over at Mia, but she was already fast asleep. Zoe's fingers were frozen in the air, unable to close themselves around the cord of the necklace.

This can't be happening. I must be so tired I'm just imagining things now. Zoe moved her hands away from the necklace. She quickly reached over to the lamp instead and turned it off. She pulled the covers up to her chin and tried to think about sleep and Noah and the Ferris wheel ride — anything but the necklace.

That night, Zoe tossed and turned. She had crazy dreams about the carnival and the Great Serafina. She dreamed Serafina was chasing her through the fun house holding a snake. Then she dreamed she was on the Ferris wheel with Noah. Suddenly, Serafina appeared in their car out of nowhere and tipped Noah out! Then Zoe had another dream in which Serafina was sitting on the branch of the tree outside her bedroom window. Her eyes were the red jewels of the pendant, and she kept chanting "Good luck, good luck," in that eerie monotone voice as the branch scraped against the glass.

The next morning, Zoe felt like she hadn't slept at all. The dreams played back through her head like a bad movie. She looked down at the necklace and hesitantly reached up to touch it. Her hand closed effortlessly around the pendant. *Okay, I must have just been really tired last night,* she thought. Now that Zoe realized she could take the necklace off if she wanted to, it didn't seem like such a big deal. Instead, she shoved the pendant under her T-shirt. Then she nudged Mia.

"Wake up, sleepyhead."

Mia groaned and slowly sat up.

"How'd you sleep?" Zoe asked.

"Like a rock!" Mia replied.

Zoe wished she could say the same.

Mia stood up and stretched. "I'm starving!"

Zoe laughed. "Let's go see what we can find."

The girls went downstairs and found a note on the kitchen table from Zoe's dad. The note was taped to a box of doughnuts.

> Dear lovely ladies,
>
> I regret to inform you that I've been called away to important business at the farmers' market. I have to pick up some shrubs for my new landscaping job. I hope you understand. To help ease the pain of my absence, I've left you a highly nutritional health food breakfast to enjoy. (Mia: Don't tell your mom.) See you in a bit. Love, Dad

"Your dad is the best," Mia said.

Zoe arranged the doughnuts on a plate and led the way to the living room. Zoe's older brother, Conner, was at basketball camp, so they had the whole house to themselves.

"He sure tries." Zoe smiled. Zoe's parents had gotten divorced when she had been in first grade. Her mom had taken a job teaching history at a small college in British Columbia, and Zoe and Conner had stayed with their dad in Portland because their mom worked really long hours and was writing an important history book in her spare time. Zoe only saw her mom a couple of times a year. Now her mom was remarried, and Zoe felt like the more time passed, the less her mom was in her life in any real kind of way. She couldn't imagine telling her mom about Noah or her film class, or anything that she really cared about. Those were things she told her dad. And she knew how hard he tried to be both parents at once.

Zoe and Mia settled on the couch and each grabbed a doughnut.

"So, we still haven't talked about what happened with Noah on the Ferris wheel last night," Mia said between bites. "I'm dying to hear the whole story!"

Zoe set down her doughnut so she could focus. "So, I told him I was glad he came," Zoe began.

"You did?" Mia exclaimed. "Nice!"

"Then he asked about my film stuff," Zoe continued. "He knew I went to camp at the Portland Art Institute this summer, so he must have been asking about me."

"Wow," Mia remarked. "Points for Tomo and Andrew for filling him in."

"Totally!" Zoe's voice bubbled with excitement. "Then he asked if he could have my number so that we could hang out again sometime."

"That's so perfect," Mia said with a sigh.

"I still can't believe how nervous I was, Mia. My face was totally on fire."

"I'm sure Noah was nervous, too," Mia said reassuringly. "He's so quiet. And I love that he gave you the bear he won at the ringtoss."

"I know!" Zoe beamed. "He's so cute."

Mia finished her second doughnut and then stood up, brushing some chocolate crumbs from her lap. "Well, I guess I should get dressed and head home. I'm supposed to help my mom clean out the garage today."

"Want me to walk you home?" Zoe asked. "I can bring my bike and ride back."

"Sure, thanks!" Mia replied.

"Okay, let me just leave a note for my dad."

Zoe and Mia strolled leisurely through their southeast Portland neighborhood. The huge trees lining the streets created a nice shade from the sun. They could hear an ice-cream truck and a few kids shouting and playing somewhere in the distance.

"So, there's something else I didn't tell you yet," Zoe started.

"Oooo!" Mia squealed. "What is it?"

"Well, when we were on the Ferris wheel last night, Noah . . ." Just as Zoe was about to tell Mia about Noah touching her hand, something caught her attention out of the corner of her eye. She looked up in time to see a giant blackbird swoop down from a tree. It was diving straight toward her!

"What the . . ." Zoe ducked down next to her bike and felt a rush of wind from the bird's wings as it flew over her. It had come within a few inches of her head. "Did you see that?"

"Yes!" Mia crouched down next to Zoe. "I think it was that big raven that's up in that pine tree now. See it?"

"Uh-huh." Zoe's heart was pounding. She felt a knot of anxiety settle in her stomach. She shaded her eyes and peered up. "It looks like it's watching us," Zoe whispered to Mia. She shivered, but she wasn't even cold.

"Come on." Mia stood up. "Let's go before it decides to dive-bomb us again."

They hurried down the sidewalk and turned onto a side street to take a shortcut to Mia's.

Zoe nervously looked over her shoulder as they walked. "That was really weird," she croaked. Her throat was dry.

"Yeah," Mia agreed with a slight shrug. "I've never seen anything like that."

Zoe couldn't help but wonder if it had something to do with the "power of the snake eye." The more Zoe thought about it, the more the woman at the carnival really creeped her out. Mia didn't seem very rattled by the whole thing though, and Zoe didn't want to make her nervous. After all, Mia was usually the one who freaked out about things, not Zoe. So Zoe decided to keep quiet about Serafina and tried to put the bird incident out of her mind.

The girls turned onto Mia's driveway and saw that Mia's mom already had half the contents of the garage spread on the lawn.

"Oh, great," Mia groaned.

"Zoe!" Mia's mom chirped from behind a mountain of stuff. She had the same small features and jet-black hair as Mia, but somehow appeared even tinier than her daughter. "Did you come to help us with our little project?"

"Uh . . ." Zoe stammered. As much as she loved Mia, helping her and Mrs. Wang clean out their garage was the absolute last thing she wanted to do on a beautiful summer day. She shot Mia a look of desperation.

"No, Mom," Mia said. "Zoe has better things to do today."

"What, honey?" Mia's mom asked absentmindedly as she arranged boxes on the lawn.

Mia rolled her eyes and Zoe giggled.

"Well, good luck," Zoe said, still laughing. Then a shiver ran up her spine as she remembered Serafina standing in the candlelight of her tent.

"We'll talk later," Mia said as she shuffled reluctantly toward the tower of boxes.

Zoe decided to ride her bike the long way home, past Laurelhurst Park. It was her favorite park in Portland, and Zoe wanted to spend as much of her sunny summer day outside as possible. As she rode, she thought about Noah. She was glad now that she hadn't had the chance to tell Mia about him touching her hand. She liked having that part to herself — at least for now.

Zoe was riding along dreamily enjoying the warm breeze when all of a sudden her handlebars jerked violently to the right. She tried to turn them and steady herself, but she no longer had control over her bike. The bike careened violently into the ditch of the vacant lot she was passing. Zoe tumbled head over heels into the dirt. She felt a sharp sting on her elbow and saw that her shorts had caught on the bike chain as she fell and were now torn at the hem. The tear looked like teeth marks from the edges of the chain. Stunned and confused, Zoe sat up. She shakily checked herself for other injuries. Other than another stinging scrape on her knee and her pounding heart, she seemed okay. The rushes of adrenaline she felt talking to Noah or riding the

Kamikaze had been fun, but the rush of adrenaline she was experiencing now was something Zoe could have done without.

Zoe pulled herself up out of the ditch and tried to dust some of the dirt from her clothes and legs. She took a deep breath and got back on her bike. She pushed off the pavement, but as soon as she was riding, the bike pitched and jerked her toward the ditch again. Zoe leaped off the bike and let it fall to the ground, her hands trembling wildly now. *What is going on?* she thought frantically.

Zoe couldn't help but wonder if this had anything to do with the woman's weird prediction. *It appears that you will make a bad decision,* she had said. *This decision may lead to some regrettable events.* Maybe falling off her bike was the "regrettable event." But what had her bad decision been? Zoe knew she could have done more to take care of her bike since she'd gotten it for her birthday. *Yes!* she thought. *That must have been what the woman was talking about! I shouldn't have left my bike out in the rain last week. Maybe it got a little rusty and that's why the handlebars got stuck. That must have been my bad decision.*

Zoe checked her pocket and realized she'd left her cell phone at home.

"Another 'bad decision,'" she mumbled to herself. With no way for her to call her dad for a ride, Zoe had to walk her bike all the way home.

Forty-five minutes later, Zoe stumbled into the driveway. Her dad looked up from his worktable in the garage and saw the bloody scrape on her knee. He ran out to meet her.

"Zoe, what happened?" he asked worriedly. He took the bike and led her into the garage.

Zoe didn't even know where to start or how to explain. She had just managed to calm herself down on the long walk home, but as soon as she saw her dad, tears welled up in her eyes and she got upset again. Why did she still feel like a baby around her dad sometimes?

"I don't know," she said. "I just couldn't control my bike. The handlebars swerved and I . . . I fell in a ditch by the park."

"Well, just sit here for a minute," her dad instructed her in a soothing voice. "Let me get something to clean up your elbow and your knee, and then we'll take a look at your bike. Okay?"

"All right," Zoe managed. She took a deep breath and tried to calm down again.

Zoe's dad returned with hydrogen peroxide and a wad of cotton balls and Band-Aids. Zoe cringed as he dabbed her cuts with peroxide. Once Zoe's wounds were taken care of, he walked over to look at her bike.

He sat on the seat and swiveled the handlebars back and forth. "Well, everything seems okay," he said. Then he kicked off and rode the bike in a circle around the driveway and came back.

"It seems fine to me," her dad said. "Maybe we should just tighten up the handlebars a little." Zoe nodded. Maybe her bike really was fine, and she had just hit a rock or something while she had been riding.

"Let me just grab a wrench," Zoe's dad said. She followed him to his tool closet. He opened the door and began rummaging around for a wrench on one of the lower shelves. Zoe heard a creaking noise above her and looked up just in time to see a hammer from the top shelf of the closet drop off the edge. She was frozen in such disbelief that she didn't think to move her foot before the head of the hammer slammed down right on her big toe.

"Owwww!" Zoe buckled, grabbing her foot.

"Zoe!" Her dad swooped down and picked up the hammer. "I'm so sorry, honey!"

"It's . . . it's . . . okay, Dad," Zoe managed in between gasps and tears. Her dad hadn't been anywhere near the top shelf of the closet! How had the hammer fallen out and hit her on the toe?

"I really need to be more careful with this stuff," Zoe's dad said apologetically.

"It's not your fault," Zoe whispered. Her knees were weak, and she felt nauseous. "I think I'll just go inside and lie down for a bit. I didn't sleep very well last night."

Zoe turned and limped toward the house, hoping her swollen toe was the last of her bad luck.

CHAPTER FOUR

Later that afternoon, Zoe hobbled into the backyard with a few supplies. In one hand she held a large icy glass of a sparkling fruit-juice concoction she'd just made in the kitchen. In the other, she carried a bag of frozen peas and a worn copy of her favorite book. A giant beach towel and a pillow were tucked under her arm.

She limped to the edge of the backyard and arranged the beach towel in the hammock. She had begged her dad for a hammock at the beginning of the summer, so she wanted to be sure he knew she was getting plenty of use out of it. And she was. Reading in the hammock was her favorite summertime activity, aside from hanging out with Mia, of course. Zoe settled into the hammock and gently placed the bag of peas over her now-purple toenail, wincing a little bit. She leaned back and positioned the pillow behind her head.

A few chapters later, Zoe's dad sauntered across the lawn.

"Hey, Zozo?"

"Yeah, Dad?" Zoe marked her place with her thumb.

"I'm going to run some errands. I'm starting a big landscaping job in Beaverton tomorrow, so I need to get a few more supplies."

"Okay."

"You all right?" her dad asked, his voice concerned. "How are your injuries?"

"They're fine," Zoe replied. "Just icing my toe and stuff."

"Well, just take it easy."

"Yes, sir." Zoe saluted and smiled.

"Oh, I almost forgot!" her dad said. "I made lasagna for dinner."

"Yes!" Zoe hooted. Lasagna was her absolute favorite. Her dad must have been feeling bad about the hammer incident.

Zoe's dad laughed. "It's in the fridge all ready to go. Can you put it in the oven at five o'clock?"

"Sure, no problem."

"Just set it to bake at three fifty, okay?" her dad instructed. "I should be home by five thirty."

"Got it, Pops."

Zoe's dad gave her a kiss on the forehead and headed into the garage. Zoe heard his truck pull out of the driveway as she set the alarm on her cell phone for five o'clock. She still had plenty of reading time before then.

When the alarm started beeping, Zoe almost fell out of the hammock. She had dozed off. She stared up through the trees at the weakening sun and took a minute to realize where she was and what the annoying sound was. She located her phone in the grass and switched off the alarm. Then she gathered up her things and headed for the kitchen. The bag of peas was a mushy, melted mess. *At least my toe feels a little better,* she thought, even though the purple was already darkening to almost black.

Zoe noticed a strange smell as soon as she opened the kitchen door. It almost smelled the way it did when her dad turned on the heat for the first time each fall. But it was way too warm outside for him to have turned on the heat today. Zoe threw her towel and book on the dining room table and glanced around the room. Everything looked normal.

She opened the refrigerator and reached in for the lasagna, but it wasn't on the top shelf. Zoe searched every shelf of the refrigerator, but the lasagna wasn't there. Maybe her dad had put it in the freezer instead. But when she searched the freezer, it wasn't there either.

The weird smell was getting worse. It smelled like something was burning. Zoe turned toward the oven and gasped. The entire inside of the oven was engulfed in flames! She had never seen anything like it. She ran to turn the oven off and stopped short. The oven wasn't even on.

"What the — ?!" Zoe whispered. What was going on? She was terrified. *It's not even on. The oven is not even* on! she repeated in her head.

Zoe spun in a circle. She didn't know what to do. *Should I call 911?* she wondered desperately. *But what if they don't get here fast enough?* Zoe stared at the oven, trying to think. Then she remembered that they had a fire extinguisher in the garage. She ran out there as fast as she could on her injured toe and grabbed it. Her heart was racing the entire time. She quickly read the instructions and decided to spray a little bit of foam on the outside of the oven before she opened the door. Then she took a pair of wooden salad tongs out of the drawer and used them to open the oven door from a distance. The second she had the door open, she showered the inside with the fire extinguisher. Luckily, the fire went out quickly but the smoke set off the fire alarm.

Zoe ran around frantically opening all the doors and windows, turning on fans and using a towel to fan the smoke toward the nearest window. Finally, the alarm stopped beeping. Zoe was sweating and disheveled. She collapsed on the floor in front of the oven, struggling to catch her breath. Once she could breathe again, Zoe peered into the oven. There was something inside. Zoe gasped. It was the charred pan of lasagna!

Zoe searched for a reasonable explanation. Had her dad changed his mind and put the lasagna in the oven before he left? No, Zoe had seen him walk straight into the garage after he spoke to her in the yard. Had Conner come home early and put it in the oven? No, he was never home from basketball camp before six. And besides, that still wouldn't explain the fact that the oven hadn't even been on when the lasagna had caught fire! It didn't make any sense. *What if someone else came into the house?* Zoe thought, her head spinning. A thick knot of fear settled in her stomach.

For the next twenty minutes, Zoe paced the kitchen, nervously twisting strands of hair around her shaking fingers. She couldn't wait for her dad to get home. When Zoe finally heard the sound of the garage door opening and her dad's truck pulling into the driveway, she heaved a sigh of relief. *Finally!* she thought. She rushed to open the door for her dad.

"Oh, Zoe!" Her dad shouted the minute he stepped into the kitchen. "What happened? Are you okay?"

Zoe burst into tears, and her dad pulled her into a big hug.

After a minute, Zoe pushed away and wiped her tearstained cheeks. "Yeah, I'm fine . . . I guess," she said, her voice wavering with exhaustion and fear. "I don't know what happened . . . I . . . the oven . . . it wasn't . . ."

"It's okay, honey — accidents happen." Zoe's dad squeezed her shoulder as he looked around the kitchen, taking in the scene. "Did you set the oven too high?"

"No, I..." Zoe started, but tears flooded her cheeks again.

"It's okay, Zoe," her dad repeated as he wiped a tear from her face with a dish towel. "You must have set the oven to broil accidentally and the lasagna just caught on fire somehow. It's a simple mistake."

"But Dad, the oven wasn't even on!" Zoe managed between ragged breaths. "I hadn't turned it on yet!"

"Honey, that's impossible," her dad said reasonably. "Did you fall asleep in your hammock again? I know you and Mia hardly sleep when she stays the night. Maybe you were still groggy and just weren't paying attention."

"No, I... well, I did fall asleep for a minute, but I swear I...I..." Zoe stammered. She could tell from the look on his face that he was sure Zoe had been mistaken about the oven.

"I'll take care of this, sweetheart," her dad said gently. "Why don't you go up to your room and relax, okay?"

"But what about the lasagna?" Zoe held out the burnt lasagna pan with one of the pot holders she'd made in Mrs. Mahoney's second-grade class. "It's ruined." She felt like she might start crying again.

"We'll just order some Chinese takeout after I get things cleaned up and Conner gets home."

Zoe sighed again. "Okay."

Zoe went upstairs and fell onto her bed. She lay motionless for a long time, staring at the ceiling as she tried to replay the events of the day in her head. First the bike, then the hammer, and now the burnt lasagna. Nothing made sense. Zoe couldn't understand why any of those things had happened — all of them seemed to be completely beyond her control. Maybe her dad was right and she was just overtired. Maybe her mind was playing tricks on her. Or maybe the woman from the carnival had been right. Everything that had happened had been a "regrettable event."

But the lasagna incident had nothing to do with Zoe leaving her bike in the rain last week. What could possibly be the bad decision that made that happen? Falling asleep in the hammock? Zoe laughed tiredly. It was all so ridiculous, but it was scary, too.

Zoe could barely finish her egg roll and kung pao chicken with broccoli. She knew her dad was worried about all the accidents she'd had that day, but Conner kept him busy with tales of suicide drills and half-court scrimmages at basketball camp. Zoe escaped to her room as soon as she could to get online. She wanted to check her e-mail and hopefully talk to Mia. Zoe set her iPod in the speaker dock and put on her favorite band. Then she started up her laptop. Her mom had a way of making up for her absence by sending expensive gifts. Zoe loved having an iPod and a computer of her own, but having a real relationship with her mom would have been worth the trade.

She opened her e-mail, and her stomach jerked when she saw Noah's name in her in-box. She did a little dance in her chair and clicked open the e-mail. Maybe this wasn't the worse day of her life after all. But when she started reading, she realized it definitely was.

zoe:

if you didn't want to hang out with me you could have just said so at the carnival last nite. you didn't have to send me an e-mail listing all the things you DON'T like about me! i'm not really sure what your problem is. don't worry — i won't call you or bother you again.

noah

Zoe's jaw dropped. She stared at the computer, rereading Noah's e-mail over and over again. Finally, she scrolled down and realized what he was reacting to: an e-mail from her. A now-familiar sick feeling crept over her as she read the words on the screen:

Noah,

I can't believe I gave you my number last night. I really don't want to hang out with you. I think you're boring and ugly and I would be embarrassed if my friends saw us together again. I don't know what I was thinking. Please don't call me. Ever.

Signed,

Zoe Margaret Coulter

Zoe put her head in her hands and groaned. Who would have played such a cruel joke on her? And who had access to her e-mail, anyway? She remembered an issue at school earlier in the spring when someone hacked into the computer system and sent fake e-mails from several of the teachers' accounts. Was there a chance this could be related? But the person would have to know what happened at the carnival just the night before! Not to mention that they knew Zoe's middle name. Only four people in the world knew that: her parents, her brother, and Mia. *Ugh, and now Noah,* Zoe thought, covering her face again. There was no way Mia would do something like this to her. Zoe thought about Conner. She jumped up from her desk and stormed down the hall to his room. She flung open his bedroom door without knocking.

"Hey, what are you doing?" Conner looked up from his computer, surprised.

"I can't believe you would do something like that to me, Conner!" Zoe shouted.

"What are you talking about? Conner demanded. He looked completely perplexed.

"You hacked into my computer and sent a prank e-mail to Noah!"

"What?" Conner asked. "Who's Noah?"

"Don't play dumb." Zoe's voice rose and faltered. "I know it was you!" Another tear slid down her cheek.

"Zoe, relax," Conner said. Zoe could tell he was trying hard to be nice. "What are you talking about?"

Zoe took a shaky breath and stared at her brother. He was leaning away from her in his chair,

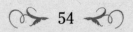

like he was afraid she might attack him. Zoe didn't know what she had been thinking. Conner had been so busy with basketball camp that summer he had probably forgotten he even had a sister — until now. And there was no reason he would have played such a mean prank on her. They hadn't had a fight in months, and he didn't even know about Noah and the carnival the previous night.

"Sorry," Zoe said quietly. "I just freaked out for a second."

"Uh, *yeah*, ya did." Conner laughed a little nervously.

"Never mind," Zoe mumbled, stepping back into the hall. She closed the door quietly behind her.

Zoe ran back to her room and logged into IM. Luckily, Mia was online. She was desperate to tell her what was happening.

Zoe503: Mia?

DancingFeet: Hey! What's going on?

Zoe503: U R NOT going to believe my day.

DancingFeet: WHAT?

Zoe503: after i left ur house i fell off my bike and into a ditch

DancingFeet: really!?

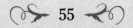

Zoe503: then a hammer fell off the shelf in the garage and onto my toe

DancingFeet: OMG! Ouch.

Zoe503: THEN i was supposed to put the lasagna in the oven at 5

DancingFeet: yum. I luv ur d's lasagna

Zoe503: i went in the house at 5 and it was already in the oven . . . ON FIRE!

DancingFeet: huh???!!??

Zoe503: the entire inside of the oven was on fire but the oven wasn't even on. seriously M. i don't know what's going on.

DancingFeet: OMG x 100! i don't get it

Zoe503: THEN (see i'm not even done yet)

DancingFeet: UGH!

Zoe503: i got an e-mail from Noah. wait i'll fwd it to u . . .

DancingFeet: Oooo! Exciting.

Zoe503: no. not exciting. bad. v. bad.

Zoe503: u get it yet?

DancingFeet: just . . .

DancingFeet: Zoe!!! Why did u write that to him?????

Zoe503: I DIDN'T!!!

DancingFeet: what do u mean?

Zoe503: at first i thot it was Conner. i just screamed at him 4 it but it wasn't him. i don't know if someone hacked my e-mail or what, but i didn't write it!

DancingFeet: Z this is crazy!!

DancingFeet: what r u going to do?

Zoe503: crawl in a hole and nvr come out? i don't know!

Zoe503: what shud i do? i am rlly freaked OUT!

DancingFeet: come over 2mrw. we'll figure it out.

DancingFeet: u ok?

Zoe503: not really, but . . . i'll b fine

DancingFeet: txt me 2mrw and u can come ovr. xoxo

Zoe503: k xxoo

Zoe clicked back over to read the e-mail one more time. She considered responding to Noah, but then she decided to wait and talk to Mia more first. Just as she was about to log off for the night another chat window popped up on her screen.

Zoe • • •

Zoe503: Mia?

Not Mia.

Zoe stared at the screen. Whoever was typing didn't even have a screen name.

Zoe503: who is this?

`A warning.`

Zoe503: Conner is that u?

`Not Conner.`

Zoe503: this isn't funny

`You are right, Zoe. It is not funny.`

Zoe's heart leaped into her throat.

`Your luck has run out, Zoe!`

Zoe's hand was shaking so hard it took her three tries to close the chat window. But she couldn't stand to see it on her screen any longer. She slammed her laptop closed without even shutting it down and flew up from her desk, her chair crashing to the floor.

"Zoe?" her dad called from the hallway. "Everything okay?"

"Fine, Dad," Zoe said, her voice trembling. "My chair just fell. I'm going to bed now."

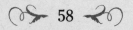

"I was coming up to see if you wanted your fortune cookie," Zoe's dad said through the door. "You left it on the table."

"Um . . . sure, okay."

Zoe opened the door and her dad handed her the cookie.

"Dad?" Zoe's voice was still shaking. "Do you believe in fortunes?"

"Only the good ones," he said as he kissed her forehead. "Sleep well, honey."

"G'night." Zoe closed the door and cracked open the cookie. She slowly unfolded the tiny slip of paper and then sank down on her bed. The message read:

TROUBLE IS BREWING. IT MIGHT BE BEST TO STAY IN BED.

CHAPTER FIVE

The next morning, Zoe woke up late. It had taken her hours to fall asleep after all of the crazy things that had happened. Sometime around three A.M. she finally dozed off, so it was almost eleven when she poked her head out of the covers.

The first thing that greeted her was the necklace that she was still wearing. She hadn't really thought about it since yesterday morning, but she still hadn't taken it off. She reached up and touched the stone for a second before she swiftly pulled it over her head and set it on the bedside table. Right away her body felt lighter, but strange, too. She realized uneasily that she didn't like not having the weight of the necklace against her chest.

Zoe ignored her feelings about the necklace and

went to take a shower. After her shower, she brushed her teeth and pulled her damp, thick brown hair into a quick braid. Then she went back to her room to get dressed.

Zoe pulled a pair of black shorts and a faded green T-shirt that read KISS ME, I'M IRISH in white letters out of her closet. As she was getting dressed, she felt numb and not at all like herself. Something weird nagged at the back of her mind. She glanced over at the necklace sitting on her bedside table, and with a jolt she suddenly knew she had to put it back on. She couldn't explain it at all, but that was the first thing that popped into her head when she saw the necklace. Somehow, Zoe got the feeling that if she didn't put the necklace back on, something terrible was going to happen. She picked it up from the table and quickly slipped it back around her neck, trying not to think about it too much. *It's just a stupid necklace,* she told herself.

She went downstairs to find the house empty. There was another note from her dad:

Morning, honey. I thought I'd let you sleep since you were so tired yesterday. Conner's at b-ball camp until six and I'll be out at

*that job in Beaverton all day. I'll check in
later. Call if you need anything. Love you!*

Zoe poured herself a bowl of cereal and sat down
at the kitchen table. She pulled her cell phone from
her shorts pocket and texted Mia: hey m wht time shud
i come ovr?

Mia texted back instantly: i'll b home frm dance @ 2.
come ovr then.

Zoe finished her cereal and went back up to her
room. She took out her fancy digital video camera
(another gift from her mom) so she could work on
her movie for a little bit. Professor Meyer at the Art
Institute camp had loved Zoe's film and wanted her
to keep working on it through the summer. Zoe was
usually super-excited to work on her film, but this
morning she felt so distracted she could barely
concentrate.

She sat on her bed with her video camera
propped on a pillow in front of her and her film notebook beside her. She decided to just flip through all
the video she had so far and write down some ideas
for what to film next.

As soon as Zoe started watching her video, it
didn't take long for her to realize that something

was seriously wrong. She was only a few minutes into the footage when giant blank spaces began to appear. Huge chunks of scenes that she'd spent days at camp planning and filming had been totally erased! Zoe let out a horrified noise — it was a sob and a scream all in one. She reversed back to the beginning and played the video again just to make sure. The dead, black screen that appeared for minutes at a time confirmed her suspicion. Zoe felt sick for the hundredth time — like a giant hole was expanding in her stomach.

The chat window from Zoe's computer screen flashed across her mind. `Your luck has run out, Zoe.` She couldn't believe this was happening. She had hoped that all the crazy things that happened the day before were just some weird fluke and that today everything would be fine. But everything was *not* fine.

Suddenly, a small ray of hope burst into her mind. Professor Meyer had a copy on disk! Zoe had given her a copy of the movie with the latest edits just last week, and Zoe hadn't worked on the film since. Zoe jumped up and fished around her desk drawer for her film camp folder. She found the phone number for Professor Meyer's office and pulled out her cell phone. She had to make sure her professor still had a copy of the movie.

Zoe paced in a tight nervous circle while she waited for Professor Meyer to answer the phone.

"This is Professor Meyer."

"Oh, Professor Meyer, I'm so glad you answered," Zoe said breathlessly. "This is Zoe Coulter from film camp."

"Hi, Zoe," Professor Meyer answered warmly. "How are you?"

"A little freaked out, actually," Zoe explained. "I was just going to work on my film, and I realized a bunch of it has somehow been erased!"

Professor Meyer gasped. "Zoe, that's terrible!"

"So, I was hoping that you still had that copy I gave you last week and that it's okay," Zoe said. "That there's nothing wrong with it."

"Yes, of course. I have it right here. Let me just pop it in my laptop and make sure it looks all right."

Zoe allowed herself to breathe for a second. Then she held her breath again while she waited for a report from the professor.

"Yep, everything looks fine, Zoe. I don't see any problems at all. I'll burn another copy and leave one with my assistant for you. You can stop by anytime."

"Thank you so much." Zoe sighed with relief.

Professor Meyer laughed. "Glad I could help. Just let me know when you're ready to discuss your new edits. I'm looking forward to it."

"Okay, thank you again. Bye."

Zoe fell onto her bed and stayed there. She didn't want to move for fear that something else might happen. Before long, she dozed off into a fitful nap.

Zoe woke up to a blast of sunlight on her face. She sat up and squinted at the oversize clock on the wall next to her desk. It was 1:52. She scrambled up and looked around her room. She was supposed to be at Mia's at two. How had she fallen asleep again when she'd just woken up at eleven? Zoe shook her head and grabbed her backpack from her closet. Then she unhooked her laptop from its charger and shoved it in her backpack. She wanted to bring it to Mia's to see if Mia could help her figure out who'd sent the super-creepy instant message and the e-mail to Noah. Mia was a total whiz with computers, and Zoe knew if anyone could figure it out, it was her best friend.

Zoe thought about bringing her video camera, too, to show Mia the film disaster, but she was still too upset to even think about that part. Zoe quickly called her dad's cell phone and left him a message that she was going to Mia's for the afternoon.

Zoe put on her backpack and her flip-flops and headed out to the garage. She faced her bike. After all the awful things that had happened, she had forgotten it had all started with her bike. She stared at the bike and hesitated for a minute before opening the garage door. She grabbed the handlebars roughly and jerked the bike toward the driveway. "Let's be nice, okay?" she told it. Zoe adjusted her helmet and climbed onto her bike. She kicked off and started cautiously down the driveway. Everything was fine. She turned onto the sidewalk and carefully set off down Alder Street toward Mia's house. *Maybe my mind was playing tricks on me,* Zoe thought. In her gut though, she knew it wasn't true. Something weird and unnatural had happened to her bike the previous day — there was no denying it.

Ten minutes later, she pulled her bike into Mia's driveway. She had been tense and on edge the whole ride over, just waiting for something bad to happen, but nothing had. Still, Zoe couldn't seem to calm the panic that was rising in her chest. Zoe parked her bike in Mia's spotless garage and rang the doorbell.

"Zoooeeee!" Mia's three-year-old sister Annabel screeched through the screen door. She jumped up and down and twirled in a circle, her thin black pigtails flopping excitedly.

"Hey, Anna B.," Zoe laughed. "Is Mia here?"

"Wanna see my new dolly?" Annabel asked, pressing her face flat against the screen.

Mia appeared behind her, opening the door for Zoe. "We have very important things to do, Anna, so we're going to my room now," Mia said officially as she grabbed Zoe by the arm.

"Bye-bye, Anna B." Zoe patted her on the head.

"Bye-bye, Zoe." Annabel pouted, letting her dolly slip to the floor.

Mia closed the door behind her and leaned on it like she wanted to be extra sure it was closed. "Phew, she's exhausting sometimes."

"Cute, but exhausting," Zoe agreed.

Zoe kicked off her flip-flops and jumped onto Mia's bed.

"Zoe!" Mia cried. "Look at your toe."

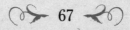

"I know." Zoe nodded as she opened her backpack and pulled out her laptop. "It looks like something out of a horror movie."

Zoe set the laptop in front of her on Mia's bed and hit the POWER button. "Maybe you'll be able to figure out how my computer got hacked, M. You're so much better with computer stuff than me." Zoe was trying hard to ignore the growing sickness she felt. It was like the hole in her stomach kept expanding out from the center of her body like a giant ball of dread. She just wanted to get to the bottom of the creepy IM and the bad e-mail. She wanted to be able to find a reasonable explanation for at least *one* of the horrible things that had happened to her in the past forty-eight hours.

Mia joined Zoe on the bed. "I still can't believe all the weird stuff that happened to you yesterday. I mean, it's crazy!"

"Tell me about it. I think I'm losing my mind or something. I hope you had a better day than I did." Zoe tried to make her voice sound normal, but she could hear the shaky edge to every word she spoke.

"Well, I had my modern dance class this morning," Mia said quickly. Her eyes were bright and it was impossible for her to hide her excitement.

"My teacher asked me to join her 'elite group' of dancers!"

"Wow, Mia, that's great," Zoe said. She tried really hard to sound excited for her friend, but she was so scared and anxious that tears welled up in her eyes instead. For some reason, Mia's happy news made Zoe feel even worse about everything that had happened the previous day.

"Zoe?" Mia asked softly. "You okay?"

Zoe wiped her eyes quickly. "Yeah, sorry. That's really awesome about your dance class," she said. "I'm sorry I'm being so weird. I just totally don't feel like myself. I'm so freaked out. I just want to figure out what's going on with my computer . . . and with my life!"

Mia squeezed Zoe's shoulder. "I don't blame you," she said sympathetically. "So, you think someone hacked into your e-mail?"

"Well, that's not all," Zoe explained as she typed in her computer password. "This morning I was watching my movie from film camp, and parts of it had been completely erased!"

Mia gasped. "Zoe! Oh no!"

Zoe swallowed back more tears. "But I haven't even gotten to the worst part yet. After we stopped chatting last night, another IM window popped up on my screen. Whoever it was didn't have a screen name or anything. The message just said, 'Your luck has run out, Zoe'!"

"Are you serious?" Mia's brown eyes widened in shock.

"It was so scary, Mia." Zoe's voice was really shaky now. "I was wondering if there was any way to tell where the chat was coming from. Here — let me log in and you can look."

"I just don't understand who would do that to you!" Mia said. There was genuine fear in her voice now, too.

"Oh no," Zoe interrupted with a groan. She covered her eyes with her fingers. Her computer was frozen on the IM page. Then, suddenly, as she and Mia watched, the screen went black. There was a tiny yellow frown face with X's for eyes in the center of the black screen. Zoe had seen that face on tech-support pages before, and she knew it wasn't good.

Zoe uncovered her eyes and leaned in to look at the screen a little bit closer. "What the...?" Under the frown face was something else. In tiny yellow type it read: GAME OVER, ZOE.

Zoe gasped and looked at Mia. Mia's face was as white as paper, but she wasn't staring at Zoe's computer — she was staring at Zoe. Zoe followed Mia's gaze and looked down at the pendant around her neck. The jewel in the center was glowing a deep and menacing red.

Zoe involuntarily reached up and cradled the pendant in her palm. Her mind felt cloudy. Hadn't she taken it off first thing that morning? Why had she decided to put the necklace back on again? Zoe tried to think, but she couldn't remember what had made her put the necklace back on.

"Zoe!" Mia shrieked. "What is going on? There is something wrong with that necklace! You have to take it off . . . NOW!" Mia was hysterical. She had leaped off the bed and was standing a good six feet away from Zoe.

"I d-don't know. . . ." Zoe stammered. Then she remembered. That morning, she had felt as though something terrible would happen if she didn't put the necklace back on. And now it seemed as though something terrible would happen if she *kept* it on. Zoe didn't know what to tell Mia.

"Take it off!" Mia shouted again.

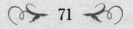

Mia's voice startled Zoe. Zoe reached up and slowly lifted the necklace off of her neck. Then she slipped it into her pocket. She silently decided that she'd put it back on when Mia wasn't looking, but even thinking this alarmed her. Mia was right — there was something horribly *wrong* with the necklace.

"What is going on, Zoe?" Mia's voice was low and serious. "This is getting really creepy. That necklace should NOT be glowing like that! It's like . . . it's like it's cursed!"

Zoe slipped her hand into her pocket again and touched the pendant. A jolt went down her spine as Serafina's voice careened through her head again.

"You don't think . . ." Zoe trailed off, shaking her head. "Well, I did have one thought, but it's just so crazy!"

"What?" Mia pressed her gently. "You know you can tell me anything, Zoe."

"Well, after I fell off my bike yesterday I thought what if . . . what if that fortune teller at the carnival was right?" Zoe finally managed to say. "What if she has something to do with all the bad stuff that's been happening to me? Remember how she said I would make a bad decision and that it would lead to regrettable events?"

"But what was your bad decision?" Mia asked, her voice rising sharply.

Zoe stared at the floor. "I should have never agreed to have my fortune read in the first place. And then I made jokes about your fortune, and asked why mine was all bad stuff. Did you see how mad she was at me?"

Mia drew in a sharp breath. "And then she did something creepy to that necklace! I *knew* she was being weird when she gave it to you."

Zoe took her hand out of her pocket. She stared at Mia, paralyzed with fear. She didn't know what to say or do next.

"Did you notice it glowing yesterday when all that bad stuff happened?" Mia asked.

"No," Zoe said. "I didn't even remember that I was wearing it until I woke up this morning."

"Really?" Mia's eyes widened again in disbelief.

"I know it's weird," Zoe admitted. "I mean, you know me — I don't even really wear jewelry. But for some reason I haven't wanted to take it off. It's really freaky."

Mia stared at Zoe intently. "We have to go back to the carnival and confront her. We have to find out what's going on!"

Zoe nodded. "You're right. This is all really starting to scare me."

Mia stood up and looked around for her shoes.

"I'll just tell my mom we're going for a bike ride in the park," Mia said. "We can ride our bikes to the fairgrounds and then straight back here afterward."

"Good idea," Zoe replied. Mia went out to find her mom while Zoe put on her flip-flops.

The girls met at the front door and ran out to their bikes. Neither of them spoke as they sped toward the carnival. *What's going to happen when we confront her?* Zoe's mind raced as quickly as she pedaled. *Will she help us? What if she makes it worse?* Suddenly, Zoe's thoughts darted back to the necklace like a magnet. She slowed her bike for a second so that Mia was riding in front of her. Then she quickly slipped the glowing pendant back around her neck, hiding it under her T-shirt. She reasoned to herself that she didn't want it to fall out of her pocket because they might need to give it back to Serafina. But she also knew that something else had made her want to put the necklace back on. Some force that she couldn't understand. Whatever it was, it made her feel sick all over again. She sped back up to Mia's side.

Before they even reached the fairgrounds, Zoe knew something was wrong. The giant Ferris wheel that should have loomed above the trees was missing. As she and Mia pedaled to a stop at the main entrance to the grounds, Zoe felt as though the wind had been knocked out of her. Where the carnival had been, there was a barren parking lot full of discarded food containers, posters, broken balloons, and forgotten prizes. Everything else was gone.

A man in dark coveralls was picking up trash near the side gate. They biked over to him.

"Excuse me," Zoe called through the fence, fear gripping her. "What happened to the carnival?"

"I can't say for sure," the man replied as he stopped and leaned against his rake.

"Wasn't it supposed to be here until tomorrow?" Mia asked, her voice tight and high-pitched.

"Yep." The man nodded. "They pulled out in the middle of the night. I came out of my trailer and they were running everywhere, packing up rides, pulling down tents. There was one woman in particular who seemed pretty ready to be on the road. She was shouting at folks to move out."

Zoe and Mia exchanged worried looks. Just then a mass of dark clouds swallowed up the sun. The sky flashed bright blue as a bolt of lightning sliced through the air on the horizon. Thunder rumbled in response, shaking the dusty ground. Zoe hadn't even noticed that the air had grown thick and heavy as they rode. Now the sky looked so ominous there was no question it was about to pour.

"Let's get out of here!" Zoe yelled to Mia over another deafening boom of thunder.

The girls hopped on their bikes and started to pedal just as the skies opened up. The rain was coming down so heavily Zoe could barely see the pavement in front of her.

CHAPTER SIX

"Zoe, over there!" Mia pointed to a run-down strip mall across the street. The girls pedaled to the other side of the road and stood under the roof of the long, narrow building.

"That looks like a bookstore down there." Zoe nodded toward the other end of the plaza. "Let's go in there until the rain stops."

Zoe and Mia locked their bikes to a post and pushed open the door of Benson's Used Books and Curio Shop. A loud chime announced their entrance. They spotted an old man hunched over a dusty counter in the front of the store. He was poring over a giant atlas. He looked up and smiled.

"Let me know if there's anything I can do for you girls," he said before going back to his map. The store was packed, floor to ceiling, with books. Along the wall behind the counter were shelves lined with old globes, statues, and other ancient-looking collectibles. Zoe couldn't tell if they were supposed to be antiques or just old junk that nobody wanted.

"We should look for a book on fortune-telling or bad luck or something while we're here," Mia suggested as she headed for the back of the store. Zoe followed Mia, straining her eyes to scan the tall shelves. The dark rain clouds outside made the dim lighting of the store even darker. Mia pulled a heavy volume off a shelf and started to flip through it. Zoe could see that the title was *A History of Magic*. Zoe moved down the row and was about to pull a book off one of the lower shelves when something caught her eye. A small, tattered leather-bound book was peeking out from under the bookcase. Zoe picked it up and dusted off the cover. She nudged Mia in the side. The cover of the book had a symbol on it that looked eerily similar to Zoe's pendant. Zoe stared at the cover. She didn't know how to feel. What did it mean? Mia grabbed the book from Zoe and opened it.

"What language is that?" Zoe asked over Mia's shoulder.

"I'm not sure," Mia mumbled, flipping through the pages. "It kind of looks like Spanish, but I can't read it, so it must be something else."

At the top of each page was the symbol from the cover of the book. "Is that the same symbol as the necklace?" Mia asked.

"Uh-huh," Zoe answered quickly. She was almost sure it was, but she was afraid to look. She didn't want Mia to see that she was wearing the necklace again.

"Need any help?" The man appeared at the end of the row.

"Do you know what language this is?" Zoe asked, holding up the book for him.

The man put on the glasses that were hanging around his neck and peered down at the pages. "That would be Italian," he replied. "I spent a bit of time in Italy a while ago. A long while ago. May I?" The man took the book from Zoe and studied it carefully. "Is this your book?" he asked.

"No . . ." Zoe answered slowly. "I just found it on the floor. It was sticking out right there." She pointed to the bottom shelf of the bookcase.

"Huh." The man scratched his white beard thoughtfully and turned the book over in his hand.

"I've never seen it before. It's definitely not in my catalog. Are you sure you found it here?"

"Yes, I'm positive." Zoe nodded, feeling light-headed.

"Zoe, we should probably go," Mia said quietly. Zoe thought it looked like the color was draining from Mia's face again.

"Yeah, we have to go," Zoe said to the store owner.

"You can keep the book if you want to." The man held the book out to Zoe. "Like I said, I've never seen it before."

"No!" Mia half shouted. "I mean, no thank you. It's okay. We don't speak Italian, anyway."

The man gave them a strange look, but Zoe and Mia scooted around him without further explanation. They ran from the store like someone was chasing them. They stopped short at the edge of the plaza and stood there catching their breath. The rain was still coming down in heavy sheets. Neither of them spoke for a long time. Then, Mia slowly lifted her finger and pointed to the top of a tree in the corner of the parking lot. In one of the highest branches of an evergreen tree sat a large, jet-black bird. A raven.

"Do you think that's the same bird?" Zoe asked, her eyes fixed on the raven. In an almost trancelike state, she reached up and pulled the necklace out from under her T-shirt. She stood, fingering the pendant gently while she stared up at the bird. "It kind of looks like the same bird. I think it's watching us again."

"Zoe!" Mia shrieked, backing away. "What are you doing? Why did you put that thing back on?"

"I . . . I don't know. . . . It just . . ." Zoe struggled to answer Mia. She couldn't explain herself. "I don't know why I put it back on. It was like some weird force came over me and *made* me."

"You have to get rid of it!" Mia sounded like she was going to cry. "Think of all the trouble it's caused already!"

"We don't know for sure it's the necklace, Mia," Zoe said, trying to reason. Even as she heard herself say the words, she knew it wasn't true. *Of course there's something wrong with the necklace,* Zoe thought. *All of the bad stuff started as soon as I put it on!*

"Zoe, it's *glowing*," Mia said sternly.

"I know," Zoe admitted, her voice a frightened whisper. "The truth is, part of me is worried that something even worse will happen if I do take it off."

Mia's eyes widened in fear. "Do you really think so?"

"I don't know," Zoe said with a sigh. "I don't know how to explain it, and I know this sounds weird, but even though I know it's bad, I don't *want* to take it off."

Zoe looked at Mia and saw true fear in her eyes. But then something in Mia's eyes changed. They darkened, and her voice was suddenly determined.

"We're going to get to the bottom of this, Zoe," Mia promised her friend. "We have to. There's no way we're letting that creepy necklace hurt you, no matter what. We'll go to the library tomorrow, and we'll do some real research on curses."

"Tomorrow?" Zoe asked. She felt tears well up for what seemed like the tenth time that day. She glanced at her phone. It was after five o'clock. "Do you think they're still open? I don't know if I can wait until tomorrow!"

"I'm pretty sure they're closed," Mia said. "But I promise we'll go first thing in the morning — as soon as they open. We're going to fix this!"

"Thanks, Mia," Zoe said. She felt a little calmer listening to Mia's confident pledge.

"Come on," Mia said. "It looks like the rain is stopping."

Zoe looked out at the parking lot. The rain was definitely lighter, and the sky looked brighter. Zoe thought she even saw the sun trying to peek through the gray clouds. Zoe hopped on her bike feeling lighter, too. She was a little surprised by how take-charge Mia was being. It wasn't like her to take the lead — that was usually Zoe's job, like with the Kamikaze. *Thank goodness for Mia,* Zoe thought as the two girls pedaled back to Mia's house. *I don't think I could handle this all on my own.*

Zoe was sure no one else would have even believed her.

"Mia, is that you?" Mia's mom called out as soon as Zoe and Mia closed Mia's front door behind them.

"Yeah, Mom, what's up?"

Mrs. Wang poked her head out of her bedroom. She was in her bathrobe, her wet hair sticking up in all directions. "Thank goodness you're home!" Mrs. Wang almost shouted in relief. "The babysitter just called and canceled on us. Can you stay home tonight to watch Annabel? Your dad and I can't miss this cocktail party. The woman throwing the party is one of my biggest clients!"

Mia glanced at Zoe. Her mom had a rule that she wasn't allowed to have friends over when she was babysitting Annabel.

"Sure, Mom," Mia responded. "Zoe and I have plans to go to the library first thing tomorrow to do some research for her film, but I'm free tonight."

"Yeah, I should probably get home for dinner," Zoe said. "Let me just go get my backpack from your room, Mia."

"Thank you, girls!" Mrs. Wang called as she disappeared into her closet.

Zoe and Mia headed upstairs.

"Maybe you should call Noah tonight to try to explain the whole e-mail thing," Mia suggested.

"I don't know," Zoe said as she packed up her computer. "Maybe I'll just e-mail him back."

"Um, Zoe?" Mia asked. "Your laptop is still dead, remember?"

Zoe laughed tiredly. She had completely forgotten. "Oh yeah. I can use my dad's computer . . . or Conner's."

"I think you should just call him. If he sees another e-mail from you he might just delete it," Mia said gently.

"Yeah, you're probably right," Zoe sighed. "I guess I'll text Tomo when I get home and see if she can get his number from Andrew."

"It will work out, Zoe. Noah's so nice, it's hard to imagine him staying mad for very long," Mia reasoned.

Mia walked Zoe to the front door. "I'll call you first thing tomorrow morning so we can make plans to meet at the library," she said. "Good luck with the phone call!"

Zoe cringed at Mia's choice of words.

"Okay, bye," Zoe said as she headed out to her bike.

Zoe rode home as quickly as she could. She just wanted to get back to the safety of her bedroom without something catastrophic happening.

She found Conner parked in front of the TV when she got home. He was eating a giant plateful of gooey chips and cheese and watching *Ninja Warrior*. "Conner's gourmet nachos," as he called them, consisted of piling a plate full of Doritos (usually Cool Ranch), adding Cheez Whiz and shredded cheddar cheese, and microwaving it for forty-five seconds. It was Conner's favorite thing in the world. Zoe thought it was disgusting.

"Enjoying your dinner?" Zoe asked as she set her backpack on the floor.

"Yesh," Conner replied through a mouthful of nachos.

"Is Dad home yet?"

"No, hesh shtill a wowk."

Zoe was pretty good at deciphering Conner's speech when he talked with his mouth full because he did it all the time, so she knew he'd said their dad was still at work.

Zoe went up to her room and collapsed on her bed. She took out her cell phone and texted Tomo. She silently hoped Tomo wouldn't write back right away, but her phone buzzed just a few minutes later.

Now that she had no more excuses, calling Noah didn't seem like such a great idea. How could she possibly explain that she hadn't written that awful e-mail? What could she say that wouldn't sound crazy? She was starting to think maybe she *was* crazy. She'd had so many weird thoughts and feelings the last couple of days she was beginning to wonder what was real and what wasn't. What if the e-mail from Noah wasn't even real? What if she called him and he had no idea what she was talking about? Then he'd really think she was weird!

Finally, Zoe took a deep breath and typed in Noah's number. She still had no idea what she was going to say, but she had been lying on her bed for at least half an hour and hadn't figured it out. So she decided to just get it over with.

"This is the last time I'm answering the phone!" Noah barked instantly.

"Uh, Noah? It's Zoe."

"Oh, so you're actually talking this time," he responded sharply.

"What do you mean?" Zoe asked, confused. "I just got your number from Tomo. I hope that's okay," she added quickly.

"I know you have my number, Zoe," Noah said. His voice was hard. "What do you want?"

Zoe had never heard Noah speak this way. He sounded so angry it scared her.

"Well, I just wanted to say I'm sorry about that e-mail," Zoe explained. Her palms were sweaty, and she was trying her best to keep her voice steady. "I'm really, really sorry. I still haven't figured out what happened, but it wasn't me. I didn't send it."

Noah laughed bitterly. "Yeah, right."

Tears stung Zoe's eyes. She couldn't believe how mean Noah was being.

"I swear, Noah," Zoe said. "I would never say those things. . . ."

"Look, just stop calling me all the time, Zoe," he interrupted her. "You're driving me crazy!"

"All the time?" The question caught in Zoe's throat.

"You can't keep calling me and hanging up. It's not like I don't know it's you. You gave me your number at the carnival, remember?"

"But this is the first time I-I've called you," Zoe stammered. "I got your number from Tomo, like, half an hour ago!"

"Zoe, stop lying!" Noah yelled. "You've called me, like, a million times since the carnival. It's driving me insane."

"But I . . . that's not true!" Zoe said. She felt a sob rising in her throat.

"You already made it clear you don't want to hang out anymore, so just leave me alone!"

The phone went dead.

Tears streamed silently down Zoe's face. She was in shock. *This is crazy!* she thought. *There's no way I*

called him before today! With shaky hands she scrolled through the dialed numbers list on her cell phone. Noah's number appeared over and over down the entire list. Some calls were only a minute apart. Zoe felt like she had a fever and chills at the same time. She threw her phone into a pile of clothes in the corner of her room. She buried her head in the arm of the stuffed bear Noah had won for her and sobbed. She could feel the pendant pressing into her chest. She pulled it out of her T-shirt and off her neck and threw it across the room. She heard it hit the floor with a thud. She rolled herself up in a cocoon of blankets and squeezed her eyes closed. *This has to be a bad dream,* she thought. *It's all just one big nightmare.*

CHAPTER SEVEN

Zoe sprang awake to the muffled sound of her cell phone ringing. *That was a terrible dream,* she thought. Zoe bolted upright in bed. It was morning. She had slept through dinner and through the entire night! She couldn't believe she'd been so exhausted. Zoe looked around her room, trying to locate her phone. She usually kept it on her night-stand, right next to the bed, but it wasn't there. Zoe's heart sank into her feet when she saw what was there. The necklace. The necklace she had thrown onto the floor the night before.

The nightmare she'd had came flooding back to her like yesterday's rainstorm. Only it wasn't actually a nightmare — those things had really hap-pened. She looked down at her scabby knee and her blackened toenail and thought of the accidents. She heard her cell phone again and thought about Noah and the phone calls. Finally, she scrambled over to the pile of dirty clothes in the corner and fished out her phone. Mia's name flashed on the screen once more and then disappeared. Zoe looked at the dialed numbers list again. Two new calls to Noah's number had been made during the night. Her stomach lurched.

She quickly texted Mia to meet her at Tropical Sunrise — their favorite smoothie place — for breakfast. Then she spotted her canvas tote bag at the edge of the clothes pile and pulled it out. She threw in her phone, wallet, library card, and after a moment of hesitation, the necklace. She put on her flip-flops and ran down the stairs two at a time. She shouted to Conner in the kitchen that she was going to meet Mia at the library and hurried out to get her bike.

Mia was waiting in front of Tropical Sunrise when Zoe arrived. "You look . . . a little disheveled," Mia remarked. "Isn't that the same T-shirt you wore yesterday?"

Zoe glanced down at her shirt and groaned. "I kinda crashed last night, and when I woke up this morning, I was so confused I totally forgot to change! Ugh."

Zoe loosened her messy braid and tried to comb through her gnarled hair with her fingers. Then she coaxed it into a ponytail. She decided to wait until they had their smoothies before she told Mia about the phone call to Noah. Mia ordered her usual Berry Blast and Zoe got her Peach Breeze. They sat down at an outside table and adjusted the umbrella to shade them from the morning sun.

"Are you ready for the latest installment of *My So-Cursed Life*?" Zoe asked glumly.

"Oh no, Zoe," Mia gasped. "There can't be more!"

"Oh, but there is," Zoe said. "And this is the worst thing so far." Zoe couldn't tell if she might burst out laughing or crying again. Zoe told Mia the story of her horrible phone call with Noah.

"But I still don't get it," Mia said when Zoe reached the end of the gruesome tale.

Zoe took a deep breath and reached into her bag. "After he yelled at me again and hung up, I looked at my numbers-dialed list." She handed Mia her phone.

Mia's jaw dropped as she scrolled through the list. "Zoe!" was all she could say.

"It's impossible, Mia," Zoe said, her head in her hands. "I mean, how could this happen?"

Mia stood up and threw her empty smoothie cup in the trash. "We have to get to the library," she said forcefully. "It has to have something to do with Serafina. We have to figure out what's happening and how we can fix it."

All Zoe could do was nod in agreement.

The girls biked to the Belmont Library as fast as they could. They locked their bikes in the rack and hurried into the computer station to look up fortune-telling, bad luck, magic, and anything else they could think of. They ended up with a stack of eight big books and sat down at a table to look them over.

A couple of hours into their search, Zoe picked up a book about curses and talismans. She had flipped through a few chapters and was about to put it down when her eyes fell on a section in the "Power Curses" chapter called the "Snake Eye Curse." She quickly scanned the pages.

"Mia, I think I found something!" she whispered.

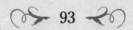

"Look at this." She pushed the book closer to Mia and pointed to the page. "Remember how Serafina said she was 'bestowing the power of the snake eye' on me?"

Zoe quietly read the page out loud.

"*'The Snake Eye is one of the most powerful curses in history. It is known to cause serious harm and injury, and can be stored in a talisman for centuries. This intense curse has the ability to choose its own victims.'*"

"Oh my gosh!" Mia exclaimed, covering her mouth after she realized how loud she had been. The librarian gave her a stern look.

Zoe continued reading, "*'The Snake Eye has been known to build in power as tragic things happen to the cursed individual. The Snake Eye also tends to create a strong hold over the unlucky soul to whom it is given.'*"

She sank down in her chair. Things were going to get even worse! And this explained why she hadn't wanted to take the necklace off. It was all part of the curse.

Mia pulled the book closer and read the next section. "*'The Snake Eye can lie dormant with an individual who has the ability to pass the curse on —*

especially someone with great telepathic or psychic energy.'"

"Serafina," Zoe whispered.

Mia continued to read aloud. "'*But even these cosmically connected individuals are not immune to its power. Without warning, the Snake Eye can control even its strongest subjects with a trancelike state, allowing its power to be forced upon new victims.*'"

Zoe gasped. "That totally explains Serafina's behavior. Her eyes got all weird and glassy at the end of my fortune!"

"Look, Zoe." Mia pointed excitedly to the next page and read, "'*There is only one spell that can break the Snake Eye Curse. It is the most potent spell of its kind: the* Incantata Zifiri.'"

Zoe perked up. "Okay, so what is it?"

"What?"

"The Incan Ziff-whatever," Zoe said eagerly. "How do we do it?"

"It doesn't say." Mia flipped ahead, intensely studying the pages. "It just goes on to describe a new curse after that. It doesn't say how to perform the spell."

Zoe plunked her head down on the tab

"Come on, let's go look on the s

maybe there's a book on spells we missed," Mia suggested, her voice rising with anticipation. This time she elicited a "shush!" from the librarian.

Mia dragged Zoe back into the stacks and combed the shelves for a spell book. Zoe slumped against the bookcase and shook her head.

"It's hopeless," she groaned. "I'm doomed. Noah is never going to speak to me again. I'm cursed! Forever!"

Mia jumped down from her step stool and shook Zoe's shoulders. "You're not doomed. We already identified the curse and the spell that can break it," she said encouragingly. "All we have to do now is find out how to do the spell!"

"This is your last warning, young lady," a firm voice at the end of the row cautioned.

"Okay, sorry," Mia yelled back. "I mean, sorry," she whispered.

The girls spent another half hour searching the catalog and the shelves for the *Incantata Zifiri* spell, but came up empty-handed. Then they waited for a computer to open up to get online. They spent another hour doing Google searches. They found several mentions of the spell on various sites and a few more facts about the snake eye curse, but nothing detailing how the spell was performed. One site even said: "Good luck finding the actual spell. I've spent years searching for it."

After they walked outside, Zoe called her dad out on his landscaping job to check in.

"Hey, Zozo. How's my girl?"

"Daaad."

"What, I can't call you 'my girl' anymore?" Zoe's dad laughed. "Seriously, Zoe, are you feeling okay? I tried to wake you for dinner last night, but you were dead to the world, so I just let you sleep."

"I'm fine, I guess." Zoe hesitated, thinking about all of the crazy stuff that had been happening. "I was just really tired. I'm with Mia at the library now, and we're going to her house to hang out."

"Okay, no problem," her dad replied.

"So I was wondering if I could just spend the night there tonight."

"Well, I'm probably going to be here a little late again tonight," her dad replied. "Maybe it would be good for you to stay at Mia's, as long as it's okay with her folks."

"Yup, they're fine with it," Zoe replied "Thanks, Dad."

"Have fun, honey, and call if you ne

"Okay, bye!"

Zoe and Mia biked back to Zoe's house to grab her things and then headed to Mia's for the night.

After the girls had spent some mandatory playtime with Annabel, Mia's dad grilled up some hamburgers for dinner. Once they had eaten, Zoe and Mia finally had a chance to retreat to Mia's room — alone.

"What are we going to do?" Zoe finally asked. They hadn't talked about the necklace or the snake eye curse since the library. "What if we can't find the spell?"

"Where's the necklace now?" Mia asked tentatively.

Zoe stared intently at her toes. "Um, well . . ." she started. Zoe decided to just retrieve the necklace from her bag rather than try to explain.

"Zoe!" Mia gasped, her voice tight and scared. "Why are you still carrying that thing around? You have to get rid of it!"

"You read that book, Mia," Zoe argued. "It said the snake eye has a strong hold over the cursed person. There's no other way to explain it. That has to be why I didn't want to take it off! I just can't *let* myself get rid of it."

Mia sighed. "I hadn't thought of it that way."

"I'm a little relieved, actually," Zoe said quietly. "I couldn't figure out why I was so drawn to this stupid necklace."

"It's just all so freaky." Mia shuddered.

Zoe shook her head. "I can't believe that woman did this to me. Why didn't the necklace send her into a trance to give the curse to someone else? Why me? I can still hear that awful robot voice of hers in my head. 'Good luck,'" Zoe mimicked in monotone.

"Well, you did kind of make fun of the whole fortune-telling thing," Mia gently reminded her.

Zoe sighed. "I know. It just all seemed so fake to me — all those bottles and vials and her accent and everything. I thought it was all an act."

"Maybe Serafina sensed that or something," Mia speculated. "Maybe the snake eye wanted to teach you a lesson that it wasn't fake."

"I've learned my lesson all right," Zoe said, her voice rising with panic. "Never make fun of something you don't understand!"

"Well, now we have to do something about it," Mia commanded. "We can't let this thing run our lives anymore!" She pounded her fist into the carpet. "Let's smash the stone or something."

Zoe turned the necklace over and over in her palm. The menacing stone continued to glow a hot and angry-looking red. Zoe swore she could even feel the heat of it deep within her hand.

"I don't think we should destroy it," she said quietly. For some unexplainable reason, she sensed that trying to smash the stone wouldn't work. Besides, what if it just made things worse?

"What if we bury it?" Mia suggested.

"Bury it?" Zoe asked, incredulous. "Where?"

"In my backyard," Mia said with a shrug. "We'll put it in a box and bury it. Maybe that will end the curse. We just need to get it away from you!"

"I don't know," Zoe started. "I mean, we just don't know enough about it yet."

"Zoe, you can't let this thing keep a hold on you." Mia was up on her feet. She charged over to her closet and started digging around. "We have to try something! We need a box."

"Here, this will do." Mia emerged from the closet and held up an old ballet-slipper box. She pushed it forward, waiting for Zoe to put in the necklace.

Zoe stared down at her palm. She had forgotten she was still holding the fiery red pendant. With a start, she realized she had been mechanically rubbing the stone between her fingers.

"Zoe!" Mia snapped her fingers in front of Zoe's face, making Zoe jump. "The necklace."

Zoe exhaled and slowly placed the necklace in the shoe box. She took the piece of tissue paper at the bottom of the box and gently folded it on top of the necklace like a blanket.

"We're not putting your favorite Barbie to bed," Mia commented wryly.

"I know. Thanks, Wang," Zoe half laughed. "I just . . . I don't know. Let's get this over with."

Mia and Zoe went out to Mia's garage and found a couple of gardening trowels and a flashlight.

"What's going on, girls?" Mia's mom peeked her head into the garage.

"Nothing, Mom," Mia answered quickly. "We're just rehearsing a scene for Zoe's next movie. We're going to be in the backyard for a bit."

"Okay, be sure to . . . Annabel, don't touch that!" Mrs. Wang turned back to the kitchen.

"Do you think we should tell your mom what's been going on?" Zoe asked tentatively. Maybe Mia's mom would know what to do.

"No way!" Mia replied instantly. "You know how distracted my mom always is. Can you imagine trying to explain *this* to her?"

Zoe nervously twisted her ponytail around her finger. "I guess you're right."

"Let's just try this first," Mia suggested.

"Okay," Zoe agreed as she gathered up the tools and followed Mia out to the corner of the lawn. Mia knelt down in the grass while Zoe stood over her, holding the flashlight and the shoe box.

"This spot should be good," Mia said as she purposefully speared the dirt with her gardening tool.

Zoe heard a noise in the tree above her head and peered up into the darkness. "Did you hear that?" she asked, her voice unsteady.

"Hear what?" Mia was distracted by digging the tiny grave.

Zoe shined the flashlight into the tree above her.

"Hey!" Mia protested. "I need that light."

Zoe heard the rustling again and moved the beam toward the noise. It was the raven! Her insides turned to ice.

"Um, Mia, you might want to hurry up," Zoe whispered. It wasn't even cold, but Zoe couldn't seem to stop her teeth from chattering with fear.

"Well, I can't hurry if I don't have any light," Mia reminded Zoe. "Why?"

Suddenly, the raven swooped down from the tree branch and dove toward Zoe. It was going straight for the box in her hand! Zoe screeched and ducked down next to Mia, tucking the box close to her body. The raven let out a loud caw as it flew back to its post.

"Was that . . . the raven?" Mia asked. Now her voice was shaking, too.

"Yes!" Zoe cried. "Hurry!"

Zoe dropped to her knees and grabbed the other trowel. Both girls dug furiously in the dirt. Mia snatched the box from Zoe's protective grasp and flung it into the hole. Zoe pushed piles of dirt on top, and Mia patted them down with the back of her trowel. They stood up and quickly stamped down the dirt as they heard the raven caw.

"Run!" Mia shouted as they dashed for the garage and the raven swooped again. Zoe slammed the door shut and locked it, just to be safe.

Mia's mom opened the kitchen door again. "Everything okay?" she asked. "I heard screaming."

"It was part of the scene we were practicing, Mom," Mia fibbed, trying to catch her breath.

"Well, I think you girls should be done with your movie for the night. And I just got out bowls for ice cream."

"Yes, we are definitely done for the night," Zoe assured her. "Thanks, Mrs. Wang."

"Thanks, Mom."

Mia closed the curtains on the kitchen window that looked out onto the backyard while Zoe washed the dirt from her hands. Then they plopped down at the table with two heaping dishes of ice cream between them. They both exhaled loudly.

"I feel better," Mia said through a spoonful of mint chip.

"Me too," Zoe lied. She didn't want to tell Mia that she still felt miserable. Burying the necklace hadn't changed the fact that something bad could still happen to her at any minute.

"I think it's all going to be fine now," Mia said with assurance.

After they finished their snack, Mia and Zoe returned to Mia's room. Zoe opened her backpack to get out her toothbrush and saw that she had a text message on her phone. She thought maybe it was her dad checking in. She flipped open her phone and stared at the number on the screen. It wasn't like any other phone number she'd seen before. It was just a string of numbers going all the way across the screen. There were no dashes and no area code — it was just a list of at least twenty random numbers. Zoe clicked on the number to open the message and felt like she had been punched in the stomach — hard. Mia was watching her with a terrified look of anticipation on her face. Zoe passed her the phone with a trembling hand. Mia looked down at the message and gasped. The screen read, YOU SHOULDN'T HAVE DONE THAT.

CHAPTER EIGHT

Zoe woke up at six the next morning. She had tossed and turned her way through another night. She was scared — really terrified — and she couldn't stop thinking about the text message. *What could possibly happen next?* she thought over and over again as she stared at the geometric shapes on Mia's bedroom wall, but she really didn't want to know the answer.

It was just beginning to get light out as Zoe lay on her stomach on the air mattress next to Mia's bed with her notebook in front of her. She thought she would try to take her mind off of everything and work on some notes for her film edits while she waited for Mia to wake up.

Zoe began doodling, her mind wandering as she tried to concentrate on ideas for her film. After what seemed like just a few minutes, Zoe realized she had completely zoned out and hadn't been thinking of anything at all — and especially not her film. She shook her head and glanced down at the paper in front of her.

Zoe gulped.

Without even realizing it, she had drawn the symbol of the snake eye over and over again. Her stomach seemed to turn upside down, and she dropped her pen in shock. She stared down at the thick, dark lines of the symbol on the page. Suddenly, something struck her. It was the same symbol that had been on the book — that small, dusty leather-bound book from the bookstore. The man had said the book was in Italian. The Great Serafina was Italian! *I come from a long line of Italian fortune-tellers,* she had told Mia. Maybe the book would give them more information about the curse! It might even contain the spell to break the curse!

Zoe sat up and stared at Mia, hoping somehow to will her awake. It didn't work. Zoe didn't want to annoy Mia by waking her up so early — she knew

Mia was just as exhausted as she was, but she also couldn't keep this new information to herself. Then she noticed just how bright Mia's room was. *Maybe it's later than I thought,* Zoe realized. *How long have I been lying here drawing this stupid symbol?*

Zoe got up and opened Mia's fuchsia-and-orange-striped curtains, flooding the room with strong sunlight. It was definitely later than she thought.

Mia opened her eyes and squinted at the sun. "What time is it?"

"I was just wondering the same thing."

Mia reached over to her alarm clock and turned the face toward her. "Whoa, it's already ten."

Zoe was floored. She really had drawn the symbol for hours, then.

"So, I had an idea." Zoe walked over and sat on the corner of Mia's bed, trying to forget about her lost morning. "You know that book we saw at the bookstore?"

"Yeah?" Mia asked hesitantly.

"It had the snake eye symbol on it, and it was in Italian."

Mia stared at Zoe with tired eyes.

"Serafina's Italian!" Zoe said. "Remember?"

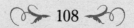

"Oh yeah." Mia seemed to be waking up a little bit at a time.

"We need to go back to the bookstore and see if that man will translate it for us. Maybe it can actually help us figure out what to do!"

"Hey, good idea!" Mia was definitely awake now.

Just then Mia's mom called them for breakfast, so they quickly got dressed and went down the hall to the kitchen.

"Don't forget you have ballet this afternoon, Mia," her mom reminded her as she consulted the calendar posted on the side of the fridge. "I have to take Annabel to swim lessons, but then I'll be back to pick you up."

"I don't think I can make it today, Mom." Mia took a bite of her egg-white omelet.

"Oh?" her mom replied. "But you never miss ballet."

"Zoe and I . . . um . . ." Mia struggled. "Uh, we're still working on that scene for Zoe's movie, and we need to shoot it today."

Zoe smiled at Mia. She knew how much Mia loved ballet. It was a big deal for her to skip class in order to help Zoe out.

"Is Ms. Durand going to be okay with that?" Mia's mom asked.

"I haven't missed a class all summer," Mia said. "I'll call her and explain."

"All right, I suppose, but just this once," Mrs. Wang said.

Zoe called her dad to check in while Mia called her ballet teacher, and then the girls set off on their bikes for the bookstore. Zoe's leg muscles burned as she pedaled. She hadn't ridden her bike this much since she'd gotten it. The late morning air was humid and there was no breeze at all. The air just hung around them like a thick, hot fog. Zoe peeled her navy blue tank top away from her already sticky skin as her mind floated back to the necklace for the hundredth time. She felt the absence of its warmth against her chest and the familiar heaviness of it hanging around her neck. She couldn't believe she actually felt this way, but she knew it meant the curse still had a powerful hold over her. And she knew she had to stop it before something truly horrible happened.

The door chime announced their entrance and they squinted into the dusty dim light of the used bookshop. Zoe let out the breath she'd been holding when she saw the man sitting behind the counter next to an old fan that was struggling to cool the space in front of it. She was worried he wouldn't be there. This time he was cleaning an old set of figurines.

"Hello again, ladies." He nodded toward them. "What brings you here on this hot morning?"

"Well," Zoe started, "we were hoping you might still have that book."

"Which book was that?"

"The one in Italian that you didn't think belonged to you," Zoe said hopefully.

"Oh, yes," he replied. "That strange little leather book."

"Yes!" Mia said eagerly. "Do you have it?"

"Well, I don't know. I don't really remember seeing it again." The man continued dusting a small porcelain elephant. "You're welcome to have a look around though."

Panic seized Zoe. What if the book was gone? It was her only hope!

Mia charged toward the back corner of the bookstore and Zoe followed. They searched the entire section three times each.

Zoe leaned against the dusty shelf and let her

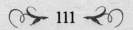

head fall back on a row of books. "It's hopeless," she said desperately.

"Don't say that!" Mia reprimanded her. "Let's look again."

This time, Zoe got down on her knees to check under the shelves but found nothing there except mountains of dust.

"Is this what you're looking for?" The man appeared at the end of the row holding the leather book in his hand.

"Yes!" Zoe jumped to her feet, her heart beating wildly. "Where did you find it?"

"Strangely enough, it was behind the counter as though it had been reserved for someone," he said. "I didn't put it there though, and I don't remember seeing it there before. Very odd."

Zoe took the book and instantly felt a searing pain in her chest where the pendant of the necklace normally lay. She gasped, trying to catch her breath, and quickly handed the book back to the store owner. As soon as the book was out of her hands, the burning sensation stopped.

Mia stared at Zoe alarmed by her reaction.

"Do you think you could translate it for us?" Zoe asked, still flinching from the book's effect. "This probably sounds silly, but we're looking for a spell to break a curse."

"I suppose I could." The man smiled and turned back toward the counter. "Let me get my glasses."

Zoe and Mia stood expectantly on the other side of the counter while the man positioned the book under a reading lamp and put on his glasses.

"Let's see here." He flipped open to the first page. "It says, '*Within these pages you will find the ancient and wise words of the Zifiri.*'"

Zoe's tired eyes grew wide. "This is it!"

The man laughed. "So this means something to you?"

"Yes, sir," Mia responded. "We need the Zifiri spell to break the curse of the snake eye, and I think it's in this book!"

The man looked back and forth between Mia's and Zoe's serious eyes. "Well then, let's have a look. Oh, and call me Mack — none of that 'sir' business."

"Okay, Mack." Zoe smiled a real smile for the first time in days. She was relieved that Mack was willing to help and didn't think they were just a couple of silly kids. They were finally getting somewhere!

"There are instructions for the most powerful spell of the Zifiri, the *Incantata Zifiri*," Mack continued.

"Yes!" Mia and Zoe said at once.

"Can you translate the spell and write it down for us?" Zoe suggested.

"Sure, sure," Mack said, reaching for a notebook and a pen.

Zoe and Mia leaned impatiently against the counter while Mack wrote down the instructions for the Zifiri spell.

"You're going to need some strange ingredients," he warned them.

"Like what?" Mia asked worriedly.

"Two raven feathers, five drops of snake venom, a strand of hair from the one who bestowed the curse, a teardrop from the one who is cursed, and the object that holds the curse within it."

Zoe let her forehead fall into her hands. "Anything else?" she asked, her face pale.

"A few more normal things, like a pinch of earth and a drop of water from a source in nature. Oh, and some candle wax."

Mack finished scribbling the instructions and tore out the sheet of paper. He handed it to Zoe and studied her face. Zoe's expression was a mixture of invigoration and exhaustion. They'd finally found the spell, but how were they going to gather all those weird ingredients?

"Anything else I can do for you?" Mack asked.

"You don't happen to have some snake venom, do you?" Zoe joked.

"Actually, I just may have something you need." Mack turned in his seat and faced the crowded shelves behind him.

Zoe and Mia stood on their toes, straining to see what he might have.

He turned back around and held out two large black feathers.

"Are these raven feathers?" Mia asked excitedly.

"They sure are," Mack told them. "There was a huge, beautiful raven hanging around the parking lot a few days ago. I happened to find these feathers when I got out of my car. I love that blue-black color, so I thought I'd keep them."

Mia and Zoe exchanged a quick look.

"Are you sure you don't mind?" Mia asked.

"They're yours," Mack said generously. "Glad I could help."

"Thank you!" Mia and Zoe said in unison.

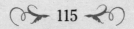

"Well, good luck," Mack said. "Stop in again and let me know how it goes."

"Okay, we will!" Zoe promised.

"And don't . . . don't get yourselves into any trouble over this, okay?" Mack added. He looked concerned.

"We won't," Mia assured him.

The girls walked quickly toward the door of the store. "Now we have to find Serafina no matter what," Mia said. "We need a piece of her hair."

"But how will we find the carnival?" Zoe asked. "They could have moved to New York by now!"

Mia stopped short and pointed straight ahead of her. She turned to Zoe and smiled brightly. "Check it out!" she practically shouted.

There was a huge, colorful poster advertising the carnival tacked to the community board on the wall next to the door.

Zoe studied the poster. "The carnival's supposed to be in Vancouver, Washington, today and tomorrow! That's not far. We can totally figure out a way to get there!"

Mia nodded. "I guess we're going to need a plan."

The girls rode their bikes toward Zoe's house with a new burst of energy and determination. Zoe couldn't believe they actually had the spell and knew where the carnival would be. It was about time for some good luck in her life! Her mind was buzzing with ideas about how to find Serafina and secure the ingredients they needed when all of a sudden she heard a loud pop. Her bike wobbled and she gripped her handlebars frantically, fearing she would be flung in the ditch at any moment. She looked down and realized she had a flat tire.

Mia slowed her bike and circled back to Zoe. "Ugh," she groaned.

Zoe crouched down to study the tire. She had just located the nail stuck in her front tire when she heard the high-pitched screeching of car tires. She looked up and drew in a quick, startled breath. A blue car in the lane closest to her was accelerating wildly. Zoe's mouth hung open and she watched with wide eyes as the car careened out of control. It was headed right for her! She wanted to move, but she didn't know which way to go. She was standing on the outside of her bike, close to the road. Zoe knew somehow that the car was going to hit her, and she was so paralyzed with fear there was nothing she could do. She closed her eyes. Then she felt something smash into her with a thud. When she opened her eyes, she was lying in the dirt on the side of the road. Mia was staring down at her with an expression of terror on her sweaty face. Mia had thrown her own bike aside and tackled Zoe, pushing her out of the way just in time. The car was about two feet away from them with its bumper resting against the curb. Zoe tried to brush the dirt from her eyes, but it was caked on with sweat. A woman in a business suit jumped out of the car and ran toward them, her hands in the air.

"Oh my goodness!" she yelled. "I don't know what happened! Are you okay? I just . . . the steering wheel seized up. I tried to turn the wheel and slam on the brakes, but nothing happened! I'm so sorry!" She was breathless and sweating even more than Mia or Zoe.

"Zoe?" Mia asked tentatively. "Are you all right?"

"I . . . I think I'm okay," Zoe eventually eked out. Her throat was so dry, it was barely a whisper.

The woman was crouched down next to Zoe. "Let me take you to a hospital or call your parents," she said.

Mia squeezed Zoe's shoulder. "Zoe, are you sure you're okay? Do you want to go to the hospital?"

Zoe sat up and looked around for a minute. Then she held out her hand for Mia to help her up. She struggled to her feet and squinted at Mia.

"I'm okay. Really."

Mia turned toward the woman, taking charge for what Zoe thought was the zillionth time in the last few days.

"We're okay," Mia said confidently. "She's fine. Nobody got hurt. It was just a weird accident."

"Are you sure?" the woman asked. She still looked incredibly worried. "I don't know what happened, I just . . . Are you sure you're both okay?"

Zoe nodded numbly, even though she wasn't okay. Physically she was fine, except for a few new scrapes to add to her old ones, but she knew it hadn't been an accident. Zoe realized the woman had nothing to do with it, but somebody — or something — had.

"Zoe?" Mia asked again. Her eyebrows crinkled into a look of painful worry.

"Really, Mia," Zoe replied. She tried to sound as normal as possible. "I'm okay. Just a little freaked out, that's all."

Mia walked back over to the woman and spoke to her while Zoe moved her bike farther away from the road and tried to clean the dirt off her face and legs. She was unable to stop tears from coming after such a close brush with danger. The woman gave Mia her phone number and glanced worriedly at Zoe a few more times, but she finally got in her car and slowly drove off down the road.

"I didn't think she was going to leave," Mia said as she walked back over to Zoe's side. "Are you *sure* you're okay?"

"Thanks to you I am!" Zoe sniffed. "Mia, you totally saved my life."

"All in a day's work." Mia tried to make her comment sound light and jokey, but the fear in her voice couldn't be masked.

"I guess I should call my dad to pick us up," Zoe managed to say through the tears streaming down her face. "I think I might need to just go home and go to bed."

"Totally," Mia agreed. "We'll figure out how to get

to the carnival tomorrow, and then we'll perform the spell and this will all be over."

Zoe nodded and wiped the tears from her cheeks. "It has to be. It's pretty clear now that the curse isn't going to stop until . . ." She couldn't even finish the sentence, but they both knew what she hadn't said. Zoe was in real danger now. She could have been killed.

Zoe called her dad. She didn't tell him about the car — only about the flat bike tire. Then she and Mia walked up to the nearest intersection and waited in silence in the shade of a bus shelter. The heat was sweltering, and they were too tired and shaken up to say much. Finally, Zoe's dad appeared in his work truck. He must have driven straight there from his landscaping job. Zoe and Mia sank into the air-conditioned cab of the truck while he put their bikes in the back.

"You girls look exhausted," Zoe's dad remarked when he climbed back in the truck.

"It's just so hot out there," Zoe replied quickly, shooting a small, knowing glance at Mia.

Zoe was just starting to nod off when her father spoke again. "Zoe, why did I get a call from Noah

Bronstein's parents this morning asking that you stop calling him?"

Zoe's heart sank into her shoes like a cement block. "Are you serious?"

"What's going on? Are you harassing this boy?" Her dad was trying not to laugh, but Zoe was angry. It wasn't funny! Nothing about this curse was funny to her.

"No!" Zoe was mortified. "It's all a big misunderstanding. I tried to explain, but Noah didn't believe me."

"Well, try to straighten things out, okay?" her dad said wearily. "I don't want to have to take your cell phone away."

Zoe sank down farther in the seat and tried not to start crying again. Mia gave her arm a sympathetic squeeze. Zoe didn't even want to look at her phone to see how many new calls had been placed to Noah.

When Zoe's dad finally pulled into their driveway after dropping Mia off at home, Zoe wasn't sure if she could make it into the house. She was so worn out from everything that had happened. She just wanted to take a cold shower and go to bed. She wearily climbed the stairs to her room and flipped on the light. She took off her dust-filled shoes and was just about to head to the bathroom when she saw something out of the corner of her eye. She turned to face her bed and let out a horrified scream. There it was — lying right in the middle of her bed: the necklace!

CHAPTER NINE

Zoe backed away from her bed. She couldn't get her breathing under control. She felt like she was going to pass out. She turned in a circle, hyperventilating now. She had no idea what to do. Should she throw the necklace out the window? Should she call Mia? Should she try to explain to her dad what had been going on?

Zoe sank to her knees on the rug in the middle of her room and pulled her cell phone out of the dusty tote bag that still hung limply from her shoulder. She tried to steady her hand long enough to punch in Mia's speed-dial number. Fresh tears streamed through the dirt on her cheeks as she waited for Mia to answer. *Pick up. Pick up!* she shouted frantically in her head, but the call went through to Mia's voice mail. She hung up without leaving a message. She knew if she tried to speak she would just start sobbing. She felt like she was having a total nervous breakdown.

Zoe stared at the necklace. The stone was still glowing — like a big red warning sign. She struggled over to her desk on her knees and searched for something to put it in. She pawed through the contents of her desk drawers as little sobs and broken gasps escaped her lips. Finally, she found an old pencil case at the bottom of a drawer. She crawled over to the side of her bed and picked up the necklace. Instantly, a feeling of calm relief washed over her. Zoe held the necklace out in front of her and hesitated. It felt so warm and inviting — like nothing bad could ever happen. "No! No! No!" Zoe shouted, vigorously fighting the urge to put it around her neck. She shook her head with quick snaps like she was trying to fling all thoughts of the necklace away from her, then she quickly put the pendant in the case and snapped it shut. She scrambled back to her desk and opened the small top drawer. She buried the pencil case under a pile of papers, closed the drawer, and used the tiny silver key to lock it. She stood up and wavered. She was dizzy and her exhausted legs could barely carry her. She stumbled to the head of her bed and put the key under her pillow.

Zoe buckled onto her bed in a terrified heap. She knew that locking up the necklace hadn't changed anything. It wouldn't stop the curse. It wouldn't protect her from further accidents. Nothing would. After all, she had helped Mia bury the necklace *in the ground*, and somehow it had still ended up back in her room like it was the most natural thing on earth — like it belonged there.

Zoe finally managed to get up and go to the bathroom to take a cold shower as she'd planned. The clean, cool water helped ease a little bit of her hysteria, but she still had no idea what to do. She returned to her room and got into bed.

The morning dawned bright and just as hot as the day before. Zoe had thrown all her blankets on the floor during the night, but she still woke up feeling sweaty and uncomfortable. She could feel the heat radiating through her wide open window. She couldn't remember another summer in Portland that had felt like this. She was surprised she had slept at all. She had expected to lie awake all night in a panic in the warm, heavy air of her room, but she had been so exhausted that sleep had eventually come, anyway.

Zoe's cell phone rang, making her jump. She was beginning to wonder if she would ever feel normal again. She reached over and grabbed it from her nightstand. Her stomach pitched a little before she saw that it was just Mia calling. She hated never knowing what to expect — that familiar sick feeling rose in her every time the phone rang.

"Hey," Zoe said groggily.

"I don't know how I missed your call last night. I didn't notice it until it was too late to call back. Everything okay?"

"No, not really," Zoe's voice wavered.

"Zoe, what now?" Mia's tone was full of fearful anticipation.

"When I got home last night, the necklace was on my bed." Zoe could barely get the words out. Saying it out loud made it feel even more real.

"No." Mia's voice was barely audible.

"I'm serious," Zoe replied. "I almost lost it."

"It's not possible." Mia sounded very far away.

"I know it isn't," Zoe said, her voice cracking again. "But is any of this possible?"

"What did you do with it?" Mia asked.

"I locked it in my desk. Not that it really matters."

"Oh, Zoe. This is terrible!" Mia sounded on the verge of tears. Zoe could tell her friend was just as tired, frustrated, and angry as she was.

"So, what time can you come over?" Zoe asked. "We *have* to get to the carnival and do the spell today."

"I have to have lunch at my grandma's house." Mia sighed. "I told my mom we have to go early so I can meet up with you as soon as we're done."

"Okay. Just call or text me as soon as you're on your way," Zoe said.

"I'll get there as soon as I can. Hang in there, Zoe." Mia tried to sound hopeful.

"I'll try."

Zoe got out of bed and looked in the mirror. She looked bad. Tired, hot, scared — just bad. She put on a pair of long, dark blue denim shorts and a white cotton sleeveless shirt with an artsy design pattern around the neck and over one shoulder. Then she went to the bathroom and washed her face and wet down the unruly curls in her hair. She tied her hair back in two loose braids and brushed a little silver eye shadow onto her eyelids, hoping to make herself look more awake.

Zoe trudged down the stairs and followed the smell of cooking bacon into the kitchen. "Good morning, sweetheart," her dad greeted her cheerfully.

Zoe kissed her dad on the cheek silently.

"You look nice," he remarked.

Zoe shrugged as she flopped down onto a bar stool.

"Everything okay?" Zoe's dad eyed her quizzically.

"It's been a rough few days," Zoe replied, unsure how much to reveal.

"Boy troubles?" Zoe's dad asked awkwardly. "Did you get that thing with Noah Bronstein straightened out yet?"

Zoe groaned. "Not yet. I don't know what's going on, Dad. My phone seriously keeps dialing his number, but it's not me doing it — I swear!" She was close to tears yet again. "Lots of weird stuff like that has been happening to me lately." Zoe watched her dad carefully, trying to gauge his reaction.

"Weird stuff, huh?" he asked, concerned.

"Yeah, like the bike accident," Zoe pointed out. "And the hammer that fell on my toe, and the flat tire, and the lasagna that burned up even though the oven wasn't on! I'm cursed, Dad!"

Mr. Coulter threw his head back and laughed. "You're cursed? Don't you think you're being a bit melodramatic, Zoe? You've just had a bit of bad luck lately. It happens to the best of us." He leaned over the bar and gave Zoe a kiss on her forehead.

She pulled away, annoyed. "I mean I *really* am cursed, Dad." Zoe's face grew hot. Her explanation had totally backfired. She thought about showing him the glowing necklace, but she knew there was no way her dad would take her seriously now. He would just have an explanation for everything.

Mr. Coulter shook his head. "You're not cursed, Zoe. You've just had a couple of accidents, that's all. Things will get better soon — you'll see. Growing up can be tough, but it will get easier. Pass me your plate."

Zoe sighed and handed over her plate. She tried hard to fight back the frustrated tears building up in her eyes. She had really hoped her dad would take her seriously. *Maybe I should have told him about that car almost hitting me yesterday,* she thought. She was so stressed and freaked out, she just wanted her dad to take control and fix everything for her. But now it was totally clear that she and Mia were on their own. No one was going to help them.

"Here you go, honey." Zoe's dad handed her a plate piled with pancakes, fresh strawberries, scrambled eggs, and bacon.

"Thanks," Zoe mumbled.

"I feel bad I've been so busy lately, so I wanted to make sure you had a nice breakfast waiting for you this morning. And I was going to suggest a do-over of that lasagna and some movies tonight."

An image of the fiery oven flashed into Zoe's head. She wasn't sure when she'd be ready for her dad's lasagna again.

"Well, I was actually hoping maybe Mia could spend the night tonight. I know we've been having a lot of sleepovers, but she's helping me with a new movie I've been working on," Zoe said.

"Yes, you certainly have had a lot of sleep-overs," Zoe's dad remarked. "I'm glad you girls are having fun."

I wouldn't exactly call it fun, Zoe thought.

"I guess that would be fine."

"Also, do you think maybe we could take the bus to Vancouver this afternoon?" Zoe asked hopefully. "I took the bus to see that video installation at the modern art museum with Makenna a few months ago, remember?"

"Vancouver?" her dad asked. "Why?"

"After we went to the carnival the other night I had an idea to shoot a movie there, but now the carnival's up in Vancouver." Zoe felt bad for lying to her dad again. She never lied to him about anything, and she didn't like doing it now.

"Let me think about it," Zoe's dad said. "Why don't you look up the bus schedule and make sure it's okay with Mia's folks and then we'll talk about it."

"Okay." Zoe breathed a sigh of relief. So far, everything was going according to plan — as long as her dad agreed to let them go to Vancouver.

*   *   *

Zoe finished her breakfast and helped her dad clean up. Then she went to his office to use his computer, since hers was still totally dead. She printed out the bus schedule and a Google map of where the carnival was supposed to be. Then she paced nervously around her room, waiting for Mia to call. She started cleaning up her dirty clothes and had even moved on to organizing her closet when her cell phone finally rang.

"Hey, I'm done. What's the plan?" Mia asked right away.

"Well, I already asked my dad if you could spend the night tonight. Do you think your parents will go for that?"

"I think it should be okay, especially since I saved the day by babysitting Annabel the other night."

"Great," Zoe said. For the first time in the last few days, Zoe felt in control of her life. She and Mia were going to break the curse. They *had* to.

"I asked my dad if we could take the bus to Vancouver to shoot a movie at the carnival," Zoe explained. "He said if it was okay with your parents, he'd think about it."

"Okay," Mia agreed. "Let me talk to my mom and call you back."

Zoe sat on her bed and waited impatiently with her cell phone in her hand. Finally, it rang again.

"I think I just signed away the rest of my summer." Mia sighed. "I have to be home first thing tomorrow morning to watch Annabel again and clean my room."

"I'm so sorry, M," Zoe said. "If you want, I'll clean your room and do your laundry and cook your family dinner for the rest of the summer." Zoe was so relieved that Mia's parents had agreed to the plan that she would have done just about anything for the Wangs.

Mia laughed, but Zoe noticed that her voice was shaky. "Let's just get this thing over with so we can actually have a 'rest of the summer'! I'll be at your house in twenty minutes."

As Zoe waited for Mia to arrive, she glanced out her bedroom window every three seconds. It was impossible for her to concentrate on anything. As soon as she saw Mia turn in to the driveway, she ran downstairs to meet her. The girls rushed back up to Zoe's room and sat on the bed with Mack's hand-written instructions for the *Incantata Zifiri*, the bus schedule, and the Google map in front of them.

"So, assuming the carnival is actually where it's

supposed to be, we have to find Serafina's tent as quickly as we can," Zoe started.

"Do you think we should just confront her when we find it?" asked Mia.

Zoe shook her head. "What if she's still in that weird trance? And if she's not, she's probably relieved to finally be rid of the curse. We'd be the last people she'd want to see!"

Mia nodded. "True."

"I think we have to sneak into the tent without her knowing." Zoe shuddered just thinking about it, but it was the only way.

Zoe read over Mack's instructions again. She alone had to perform the spell. The instructions made it clear that only the cursed individual could do it. So, once they had all the ingredients on the list, Zoe needed to combine them in a specific order exactly one hour before sunset. Then there was a chant Zoe had to say and instructions for destroying the talisman of the curse — the necklace.

"I think we should just get to Vancouver as quickly as we can so we can get back to my house to do the spell tonight. I looked online and the sun sets at 8:08, so that means I have to perform the spell at exactly 7:08."

"Okay, that sounds good, I guess," Mia agreed meekly. "But what about the snake venom? Where are we going to find that?" Zoe could tell Mia was growing more and more nervous about their plan.

Zoe, on the other hand, was starting to feel some of her old confidence coming back. She knew this was their only chance to break the spell, and she was willing to do whatever it took.

"Well, while I was waiting for you to get here I remembered something I saw in Serafina's tent. There was a snake head in the corner with its jaws open like it was about to strike. It was super-creepy. That should have been the first clue that I was about to make a bad decision!" Zoe sighed. "Anyway, there was a tiny glass vial in the snake's jaws. That *has* to be snake venom, right?"

"Probably . . . maybe . . . I don't know," Mia responded tensely.

"So, first we have to get to Vancouver without anything horrible happening," Zoe continued.

Mia fell back on the bed, covering her face with her hands.

"Then we have to sneak into Serafina's tent and steal the snake venom from the snake's jaws and find a strand of her hair."

Mia groaned.

"Then we have to get out of the tent without getting caught."

"Ugh," Mia responded. "I'm sick to my stomach just thinking about it."

"I know," Zoe agreed. "And then after that, we have to get back here in time to do the spell an hour before sunset."

Zoe fell back on the bed next to Mia and tried to breathe. So many things could go wrong. And what if they didn't even make it to the carnival *or* to Serafina's tent? What if their bus ran off the bridge into the river before they even got to Vancouver? After the car accident yesterday, Zoe couldn't stop her mind from going in a million tragedy-filled directions.

After a while Mia broke the silence with another question. "So how are we even going to get into her tent in the first place?"

The girls fell silent again.

"What if you wear some sort of disguise and distract Serafina while I sneak into the tent?" Zoe finally suggested.

"You can't be serious!" Mia sat up, a horrified look on her face.

"Why not?"

"Why not?" Mia screeched. "What if she knows it's me? What if she traps me in a cage and makes me her slave? Or worse — what if she curses me, too?"

"You won't get caught," Zoe said confidently. "We'll make the disguise really good. We'll make you look like a boy. We can pull it off with some of my brother's clothes and stuff."

Mia covered her face again.

"What else are we going to do?" Zoe pleaded. "She can't know that we're there."

Mia uncovered her face and nodded a small, reluctant nod. "Okay, fine."

"Great!" Zoe jumped up. "You work on fixing your hair and I'll go raid my brother's closet and talk to my dad about the bus schedule."

Zoe returned twenty minutes later with an armload of clothes.

"So, there's a bus that leaves Portland at 3:15. My dad said he would drive us to the bus station, make sure we get on the right bus, and then pick us up from the 6:05 bus back from Vancouver. We just have to remember to call him when we get there and then again when we get on the bus to come back."

"All right," Mia responded. She seemed distracted as she tried to pin her long hair up to lay flat against her head.

"Here," Zoe handed her a hat. "I brought you one of my brother's baseball caps."

"Thanks, that will help," Mia said as she stuffed her long hair into the cap.

Zoe also gave Mia a Portland Trailblazers T-shirt and a pair of cargo shorts. "Luckily, this T-shirt shrunk, so it won't be too enormous on you. The shorts though, are probably going to look like pants."

Mia gave Zoe a doubtful look.

"We'll just have to cinch them really tight with a belt."

Mia changed into her outfit, and Zoe surveyed the costume seriously.

"Are you sure about this?" Mia asked, clearly not sure herself.

"I think it actually works. You have sneakers to wear and the baseball cap totally covers your hair. You really look like a boy!" Zoe said, actually smiling a bit at their handiwork.

"Okay, let's go get this over with." Mia said. "We can figure out the rest of the plan on the bus."

CHAPTER TEN

Zoe's dad gave them a confused look when he saw Mia.

"Mia has to play the role of a boy in the scene we're shooting at the carnival," Zoe explained. "Do you think she passes for a boy?"

"I guess so." Zoe's dad laughed. "You're one dedicated actor, Mia."

"Tell me about it," Mia mumbled.

Zoe's dad went over his safety speech one more time before Zoe and Mia jumped on Bus 106 to Vancouver.

They settled into seats at the back of the bus and devised the rest of their plan. Zoe even had brought a notebook so they could sketch things out.

It really was like they were planning a scene for a movie.

"Once we get close to the fairgrounds, we'll separate so no one even sees us together," Zoe started. "Then whoever finds Serafina's tent first will text the other one."

"Okay," Mia responded. "So, once we know where her tent is, how am I going to distract her?"

"What if you just keep walking back and forth outside her tent calling someone's name?" Zoe suggested. "Like you can't find your friend or something?"

"And then what?"

"Hopefully, she'll come out of the tent and ask you what you're doing. You could say that you can't find your friend and don't know how to get back to the ride where you were supposed to meet. Then say the name of the ride that's farthest away from her tent. Maybe you can even get her to lead you to it."

"Hmmmm." Mia considered the plan. "I guess that might work."

The girls looked out the window as they crossed the river.

Zoe quickly turned back to Mia and focused on her face, trying to ignore the fact that their bus was over the water now.

"But what if she won't show me where to go?" Mia asked.

Zoe was silent for a few minutes. *This* has *to work,* she thought frantically. Then suddenly it came to her.

"Can you fake cry?" Zoe asked.

Mia took a deep breath. "I can try."

"I think that might help. And maybe if you tell her you can't find your mom instead of your friend that will make it more believable — especially since you look pretty young with that hat on."

"Okay, so I act upset and start crying outside the tent and hopefully she comes out," Mia started to recap. "When she does, I tell her that I was supposed to meet my mom near whatever ride is farthest away, except that I got lost. And then I'll just play up that my mom will be upset that I wandered off by myself. Maybe that will make her feel obligated to lead me to the ride."

"Perfect," Zoe said just as the bus pulled into the terminal. Zoe took the printed Google map out of her tote bag and studied it as they left the bus. They set off in the direction of the fairgrounds — luckily, it was within walking distance.

"Call your dad," Mia instructed Zoe.

"Oh yeah," Zoe said. She was so focused on their plan and so nervous about sneaking into Serafina's tent that she had already forgotten her dad's instructions. She could feel her pulse accelerating, and they hadn't even reached the carnival yet.

Zoe and Mia held their breath as they neared the fairgrounds. All their planning wouldn't matter if the carnival wasn't even there. Mia grabbed Zoe's arm and pointed at the sky. They could just see the top of the Kamikaze above the building in front of them. Zoe squealed and jumped around, totally relieved. Maybe her luck really was about to change!

They decided to part ways a block before the carnival entrance. Mia went around toward the right-hand side to try to find a separate entrance while Zoe walked toward the main gate. She passed by the ticket window and entered the carnival. Luckily, she didn't have to pay an entrance fee just to walk around. Zoe put on the baseball cap she had also brought in case Serafina happened to be out of her tent and recognized her. She kept her eyes shaded and didn't make eye contact with anyone as she searched for the tent.

Zoe walked the rows of the carnival for about five or ten minutes when her cell phone buzzed that she had a text message. It was Mia. Fnd it! Near rt side entrce.

Zoe started walking toward the far right entrance to the grounds and then ducked behind a row of porta-potties to call Mia.

"So, could you tell if she was inside?" Zoe asked when Mia answered.

"Yes! I actually saw her walk in and she was alone. It looked like she was coming back from filling a jug of water or something. And I figured out which ride is farthest away from here, so I'm as ready as I'll ever be," Mia said all in a nervous rush.

"Great! I'll head over there," Zoe said. "As soon as I find the tent and somewhere to hide so I can see whether or not she goes with you, I'll text you."

"Okay."

"Hey, Mia?"

"Yeah."

"You're the best BFF ever."

"And don't you forget it!"

Zoe hurried toward the edge of the carnival and scanned quickly for the tent. They had to work fast to make it back in time for their bus. If they missed it, Zoe had a feeling her dad would not be so accommodating regarding the rest of her summer plans. Finally, she spotted the tent. Just seeing it brought the night of the carnival flooding back to her mind. She could smell the heavy perfume of the candles, and she could see the woman's translucent eyes staring right through her as she delivered the curse. Zoe shivered with dread. She couldn't wait until this was all over.

Zoe scurried to the back side of the tent and looked around for somewhere to hide. There was a flat trailer parked about a hundred feet away from the tent with several cars from one of the rides resting on the back of it. Zoe made sure no one was looking and then ran over and climbed into one of the cars. She could easily see the front of the tent but stay hidden in the car at the same time. She crouched down and texted Mia. Ready.

A minute later, Mia appeared in front of the tent. She paced back and forth a few times and made a loud sniffling sound. Then she blew her nose and made a little squeaking noise. Zoe was impressed by how real it seemed. Just then the flap of Serafina's tent opened a few inches. Zoe felt sick. She swore she could feel the heat from the absent necklace on her chest.

Serafina stepped out of the tent and walked slowly toward Mia with her arm out. Zoe smiled. It looked like she might actually buy Mia's act. Zoe could see the woman's dark eyebrows and catlike eyes as she talked to Mia. Mia kept her head down and stared at the ground whenever she answered Serafina's questions. Zoe couldn't hear what they were saying, but Serafina put her hand on Mia's shoulder. *It's working!* Zoe thought. Now she needed to be ready the minute they walked away.

Mia pointed vaguely toward the other side of the carnival, and Serafina looked in that direction. Then she looked back toward her tent and it seemed like she was changing her mind. Mia sensed her hesitation and quickly put her head in her hands and acted like she was crying again. Zoe could swear she really was.

Finally, after what seemed like an eternity, Serafina made a move toward the other side of the grounds with Mia, but then she stopped.

"No!" Zoe whispered.

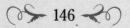

Serafina turned and walked back toward her tent. Mia looked around, trying to see if she could spot Zoe. Zoe ducked down. She didn't want Mia to see her — Serafina might catch a glimpse of her wandering gaze and get suspicious.

After a few moments, Zoe peeked out and saw that Serafina had just gone back to close the front of her tent. She really was going to walk with Mia toward the other side of the carnival! Zoe was so relieved she thought she might cry. She almost couldn't believe that their plan might actually work. Zoe waited until they turned around the edge of a trailer parked farther down the row. Then she shot out of the car and across the open lot. She looked quickly in both directions and ducked into the tent. Her heart was pounding so hard the pressure pulsed against her eardrums.

She looked frantically around the small space. "Okay, snake venom and Serafina's hair," Zoe reminded herself. "Find the snake head first." She scanned the cot and the table next to it where the snake head had been. She didn't see it anywhere. She dropped down on her knees and started to crawl across the floor of the tent, covering every inch. There was a worn leather bag shoved under the cot, and Zoe struggled to pull it out. There were mostly clothes inside, but Zoe dug crazily through the bag looking for anything else. She felt something hard against her hand and found an interior zipper pocket in the bag. There was a small toiletry bag inside. She opened the bag and found a hairbrush! She made an "ew" face and then grabbed the brush and pulled out all the hair she could see and put it in the plastic bag she had waiting in her tote bag.

"One down," she whispered quietly to herself. Her heart was beating so loudly Zoe could barely hear her own thoughts.

Next, Zoe shuffled on her knees back toward the table in the center of the room. She could only see candles and tarot cards there. She inched around the edge of the table, desperately searching the ground. Just then she heard talking outside the tent. It sounded pretty far away, but it was getting closer.

Zoe felt like she was going to pass out. If Serafina found her in the tent, what would she do? She was already cursed — could she make the curse even worse than it was? Zoe strained to hear the voices, but couldn't make them out. She lunged toward the side of the tent and sifted through another small bag — it was just full of more candles. But then Zoe remembered the spell called for candle wax, too. She shoved one of the candles in her tote bag.

She spun around in a panic. There weren't many more places she could look in the small space. She was about to give up and run out of the tent when something caught her eye. In the far corner, behind a jug of water, was a small wooden box. She grabbed for the box and pried the lid off. The snake head was nestled gently inside on the same bed of red satin Zoe had seen before. A small vial of liquid was positioned perfectly between its outstretched jaws. This had to be the snake venom. If it wasn't — well, Zoe didn't want to think about the alternative. Zoe reached into the snake's mouth with two fingers and made another "ew" face. She cautiously removed the vial as if the snake might clamp down on her fingers any second. She carefully put the vial in her shorts pocket and turned toward the entrance to the tent. Then she heard the voices again. They were right outside the tent!

". . . just a child who'd lost his mother."

It was Serafina!

"I have a bad feeling about this place, Frank," Serafina continued.

"You said that about Portland, too," a male voice responded.

"Something isn't right here," Serafina spoke again. "The energy is bad. We need to head back east and get away from this area."

So Serafina really had been responsible for the carnival leaving Portland early! *She must be trying to get away from the curse as quickly as she can,* Zoe thought.

"We can't skip out on every town in the northwest just because you have a bad feeling, Sera," the guy, Frank, spoke sternly. "Besides, the boss was angry enough about losing a night in Portland. He's beginning to think your premonition was fake."

Zoe spun toward the back of the tent and looked desperately for somewhere to hide. There was no way she was going to let Serafina find her there. She was about to dive under the cot when a shadow of light on the ground caught her attention. She realized there was a small slit in the back of the canvas that had been opened farther. She moved closer and could see Mia's hand poke through the opening. She was frantically motioning for Zoe to squeeze through.

"It was not *fake*, Frank," Serafina hissed. "There's danger here!"

"Well, I guess we'll talk to the boss about it in the morning." Frank sighed.

"All right, fine," Zoe heard Serafina say. "Good night, Frank." The front of the tent rustled.

Zoe held her breath and flew toward the back of the tent. She practically somersaulted through the space Mia had made. She heard the canvas rip a bit more around her. She was shaking so much she could hardly stand up, but Mia grabbed her arm and led her toward the side of another trailer that was parked behind the tent. The girls hid there for a minute and waited, trying to catch their breath.

Zoe couldn't believe she had actually done it. She'd found the ingredients they needed and got out without Serafina catching her. And yet she couldn't escape the feeling that something horrible could still happen. They just needed to get back to her house and do the spell. She wouldn't feel safe until they did.

Mia peeked out from their hiding place and tried to listen or watch for any movement from Serafina's tent or the area around it. After another torturous minute, she finally motioned for Zoe to follow her. Mia pointed silently in the direction she thought they should go — sticking to the back of a row of trailers until they could dart out of the side entrance of the fairgrounds. Zoe swallowed hard and nodded that she would follow Mia. *Please, please, please,* Zoe silently pleaded, *don't let anyone see us.*

Mia got to her feet, glanced one last time toward the tent, and then bolted down the row of trailers. Zoe didn't even look in the direction of the tent — she just focused on Mia and ran as fast as she could toward the exit in front of them.

The girls didn't stop running until they reached the bus station. Still trying to catch her breath, Zoe scanned the bus departure screen to locate Bus 219 to Portland. Then she and Mia sprinted to the gate. They reached the bus just as the door was closing. Zoe pounded on the glass and the annoyed driver reluctantly opened the door for them to climb inside.

Mia stumbled to the very back of the bus and collapsed into the window seat. Zoe followed behind and practically dissolved into the seat next to her. Zoe was so relieved to be away from Serafina and the carnival, but a new fear was creeping into her thoughts.

"What if the spell doesn't work?" she said. She couldn't keep this new worry to herself.

"It has to," Mia croaked. Zoe could hear the exhaustion in her voice.

Zoe exhaled and closed her eyes. *It has to,* she thought.

CHAPTER ELEVEN

Zoe's dad was waiting when the bus pulled up at 6:31. They had almost forty minutes before the spell needed to be performed. *I hope we have enough time to get ready,* Zoe thought. She didn't think she could make it through another day under the curse, so they had to do the spell tonight.

Zoe talked quickly and quietly as they walked to her dad's truck. "So, we have the venom, the feathers, the hair, and the candle wax."

Mia looked confused.

"I took one of Serafina's candles, too. I thought it would help to have as many of her things as possible."

"Good thinking."

"We just need some dirt and some water."

"And one of your tears."

"What?"

"That's one of the ingredients on the list. A teardrop from the person who's cursed," Mia reminded her.

"Oh yeah, right," Zoe replied. "I guess we'll have to figure that out."

"How did the scene shoot go?" Zoe's dad asked when they climbed in the truck.

"Good," they both answered exhaustedly.

"How was your part as the male lead, Mia?"

"Um . . . fine, I guess," Mia said, stealing a glance at Zoe.

"She's being modest, Dad," Zoe added. "She was amazing! It was totally an Oscar-worthy performance."

"Glad to hear it," Zoe's dad said, stifling a laugh.

When they reached her house, Zoe checked the time on her phone. 6:48. They only had twenty minutes before they had to perform the spell.

"Thanks again, Dad!" Zoe called as she leaped from the truck and ran into the house.

"Yeah, thanks!" Mia echoed.

They flew up to Zoe's room and laid out the ingredients on the rug. Then Zoe consulted Mack's list.

"Okay, you go out to the backyard and get the dirt and I'll get the water from the kitchen," Zoe instructed Mia.

"But I thought the water had to be from 'in nature' or something weird like that. I don't think we can use water from the tap," Mia argued.

Zoe sat back on her heels. "Good point. Hey, there's that little fountain my dad made out of rocks in the backyard. That's 'in nature,' right?"

"True," Mia nodded. "Let's try it!"

"Okay, so you get the dirt and water from the backyard and I'll get the other stuff."

Mia jumped up and ran out. Zoe quickly followed. She needed to get a bowl, a book of matches, a cup to collect her tears, and a hammer from the garage. Then she had to figure out how to make herself cry.

"What's going on now?" Zoe's dad looked up from the baseball game on TV.

"We're just working on some final things we need to film, Dad," Zoe tried to use her innocent voice again. "No big deal."

Zoe's dad sighed. "Well, try not to break anything. You seem to be a little accident-prone lately."

"Um, yeah, okay," Zoe replied, but she noticed that her dad's eyes were back on the baseball game. Perfect!

Mia came in from the backyard holding a bag of dirt and a cup of water, and the girls ran back to Zoe's room. Zoe took the key out from under her pillow and faced the desk. She prayed silently that the necklace was still there as she unlocked the drawer and took out the pencil case. With shaky hands she opened the case and stared down at the menacing pendant. She could see the red glow intensify as soon as she opened the case. She walked back to the rug where Mia was waiting and added the necklace to the rest of the ingredients. It was 6:59.

"So, I think we have everything except your tears, right?" Mia asked.

"Yeah. I haven't exactly figured that part out yet," Zoe said.

"Just think about everything that has happened," Mia suggested. "That should be enough to make you cry."

Zoe sat down on the rug and focused on the events of the last few days. The carnival had been the most fun ever, and Noah totally liked her! And then everything had crash-landed into the worst time of her life. Noah might never speak to her again. Her computer was dead, her film had been ruined, and she had almost been hit by a car.

Before long, silent tears began to stream down her tired face. Tears were welling up in Mia's eyes, too, as she handed Zoe the cup to catch the drops. Zoe tipped her head forward and watched the tears splash into the glass. Then she looked at the giant wall clock by her desk. It was 7:05. She had to stop crying now. She had less than three minutes before she needed to start the spell. Zoe took a deep breath and wiped her face. She studied the instructions again. Mia laid each of the ingredients in the order it was needed. Neither of them would touch the necklace — they just pushed it around in the pencil case. Then Zoe lit the candle so the wax would be ready to drip onto the mixture.

"What if your dad walks in or something?" Mia asked nervously.

"He won't," Zoe replied. "He always knocks. And besides, the baseball game is on, so he's glued to the TV, anyway."

The clock turned to 7:07. Zoe held her breath for what seemed like the longest minute of her life. 7:08.

Her stomach dropped. This was it. She exhaled a tired, worried sigh and nodded at Mia. Mia tried to smile but she was so nervous it looked more like a grimace of pain. It was time for Zoe to begin the spell.

Zoe placed the two raven feathers at the bottom of the bowl, forming an X. Then she dripped ten drops of candle wax over the feathers in a counter-clockwise motion. Her hand was surprisingly steady as she moved it over the bowl. Next, she mixed a pinch of dirt and five droplets of water and poured that in the bowl. Then Serafina's hair was added to the pile. Zoe's teardrop was the next ingredient. Zoe held the cup over the bowl and let one drop fall on top of the other ingredients.

The last two ingredients were the necklace and the snake venom. Zoe picked up the necklace from the pencil case and quickly placed it in the bowl before it could grab a hold of her thoughts again. The glow of the red stone began to pulsate wildly as soon as it touched the bowl. Zoe and Mia stared at the jewel with a mixture of horror and fascination. Finally, Zoe picked up the vial of snake venom and carefully removed the stopper. Now came the chant. Zoe had to say the chant in Italian as she spilled five droplets of venom onto the snake eye pendant — this time in a clockwise motion. Luckily, Mack had written out the easiest way to pronounce the Italian words. Mia held the piece of paper out in front of Zoe while Zoe positioned the venom vial over the bowl. Slowly, she pronounced each word as best she could.

Un serpente, senza una lingua,

(A snake, without a tongue,)

Un serpente, senza veleno,

(A snake, without venom,)

Un serpente, senza un occhio,

(A snake, without an eye,)

La maledizione è rotta.

(The curse is broken.)

Zoe let the drops of venom fall gradually into the bowl. She was careful to make sure she added exactly five drops.

Once the venom was added and the chant was finished, she had to say it again four more times while moving her left hand over the top of the bowl. Each time she finished the chant, Zoe could see the glow of the stone getting fainter and fainter. She started chanting louder and with more confidence. The spell was working! As soon as the chant left Zoe's lips for the last time, the pendant stopped glowing completely. The stone looked thick and black. She couldn't see through it at all anymore.

"It's working," Mia whispered, her voice full of awe. "I can't believe it's really working!"

"Shh!" Zoe said gently. "Let's not jinx anything!"

The final step of the spell was to destroy the talisman of the curse. Zoe and Mia had decided Zoe should smash the pendant with a hammer and cut the cord of the necklace. Zoe used the edge of a kitchen towel to remove the pendant from the bowl. She didn't want the necklace to touch her skin ever again. And besides, now it was covered in snake venom and Serafina's hair. Gross.

Zoe placed the necklace on the towel and folded the towel over the pendant. She positioned the hammer over the center of the pendant. Then she grinned at Mia and brought the hammer down — hard. She could hear the pendant crack under the blow. Zoe swung the hammer down a few more times for good measure, feeling herself relax a little more with every whack. Then she carefully lifted the towel. The metal pendant was unrecognizable, and the black stone was smashed into hundreds of tiny pieces — like black sand.

Suddenly, the pieces of stone began to shake and swirl. They formed a mini tornado of black dust hovering slightly above the towel. Zoe and Mia stared at the swirling cloud in disbelief. Without really knowing why, Zoe picked up the half-empty vial of snake venom and removed the stopper again. She brought it down close to the towel. The funnel cloud of stone dust swirled toward the vial and then snaked its way inside. As soon as the last piece of the stone entered the vial, Zoe quickly put the stopper back in. The dust mixed with the venom and turned to a black, gooey tarlike substance.

Zoe placed the vial on the towel next to the cut leather cord and the scattered pieces of metal. She gathered up the edges of the towel. "Let's bury it in the yard," she suggested. "I have a feeling this time it won't go anywhere."

"Good idea," Mia agreed.

Zoe added the leftover spell ingredients to the towel. She took the bowl downstairs to wash it and to tell her dad they were going out to the backyard for a minute. He just nodded his head and went back to the game.

Mia brought the towel down to the kitchen and they went out to the garage to get a shovel.

"I can't believe it worked!" Zoe laughed. She felt light and free and happy again for the first time in days. Zoe couldn't explain it, but she just knew the spell had worked and the curse had been broken. The oppressive cloud that had hung over her for days was gone.

With a sudden burst of energy, Zoe dug the hole in no time. She made it extra deep so her dad wouldn't stumble upon the weird mixture of things if he decided to plant anything new in the yard. Mia opened the towel and dumped the bad luck inside. Both girls spit into the hole for good measure, and then Zoe quickly filled in the dirt and stamped it down. The girls ran back inside.

Zoe's dad was just getting out plates for dinner. He had made lasagna. Zoe smiled. Suddenly, she realized how starving she was. Lasagna sounded perfect. She gave her dad a hug. "We're done running around, Dad," she told him. "And things are going to be totally normal from now on, I promise."

CHAPTER TWELVE

Zoe was just dozing off in her hammock with a book slowly sliding from her fingers when her cell phone rang. She reached into the grass to grab it and squinted at the screen. It was Noah.

"Hi, Noah," Zoe answered.

"Hey," Noah replied. "So, um . . . I was wondering if maybe . . . um, if you're not busy or anything . . . but if you are it's no big deal, we can do it another time, but . . . do you want to go to the movies tonight?"

Zoe smiled and wiggled excitedly in the hammock. "Sure, yeah. That sounds fun!"

"Okay, great!" Noah said enthusiastically.

Zoe scrunched her eyes closed and felt her face getting hot, even though she was alone in her backyard. Noah and Zoe had been back on speaking terms for about a week, but their phone conversations were still more than a little awkward. Zoe hoped they would feel more comfortable by the time school started next week.

"So, Zack wants to come, too, and he asked me to ask you to invite Mia," Noah said.

Zoe lifted her eyebrows in surprise and then smiled again. Zack liked Mia! She couldn't wait to tell her. Mia was due to arrive at her house any minute.

"Totally!" Zoe replied excitedly. "She's on her way to my house right now, so I'll ask her and then I'll call you back."

"Okay, bye!" Noah said quickly.

Zoe giggled. "'Kay, bye."

Just then Mia appeared in the kitchen doorway. "Hey!"

"Oh my gosh, Mia!" Zoe struggled out of the hammock and dashed toward her. "Zack wants to know if you want to go to the movies tonight!"

"Really?" Mia's face lit up.

"Yes! With me and Noah!"

Zoe and Mia ran back to sit sideways in the hammock and make a plan for their date. Everything had not only returned to normal as soon as they'd performed the spell and destroyed the necklace, but it seemed that things were better than ever. It did take a few days for Noah to come around, though. Zoe had a hard time even getting his number at first — his parents had made him change it because of all her calls, and she had been super-embarrassed the first few times she had called.

Once Noah was willing to speak to Zoe again, she convinced him to let her and Mia come over to his house and tell him the whole story. They hadn't told anyone else what had happened. Noah was the first and only person to hear all about the curse. After Noah had heard everything, they made him come with them to the bookstore. They wanted to thank Mack for his help with the spell and show Noah the book with the snake eye symbol on it. Mack was happy to see them and hear that the spell had been successful, but he didn't have the book anymore. He said the very next day when he opened the shop he looked everywhere for the book and it was nowhere to be found. He told them he'd looked every day since then, and it had never turned up.

Mack's story seemed to help Zoe's case with Noah. He wanted to know all the details of the spell and hear again how Zoe snuck into Serafina's tent at the carnival.

Zoe's computer was fixed, all her wounds were healed, her film was restored, and Professor Meyer had loved her new idea for a short film about a girl who's been cursed. And now Noah had called to ask her out! Things were definitely looking up.

"So, I have a little present for you." Mia reached into her pocket and handed something to Zoe.

Zoe gasped. "Mia, it's beautiful!" She held up the delicate silver necklace with one tiny charm dangling from it: a four-leaf clover.

"I thought you could use a good luck charm to seal your *real* fortune." Mia grinned.

"I love it!" Zoe fastened the necklace around her neck and marveled at how light it felt. "It's perfect, Mia. Thank you so much."

Mia and Zoe swung back and forth in the hammock.

"I can't believe we're going to the movies with Noah and Zack," Mia said.

"I know." Zoe beamed. "I think it's safe to say my luck has changed."

Just then they heard a rustling in the leaves above their heads. Zoe strained to see into the tree.

"Mia, look!" she whispered. It was a giant black bird, and it seemed to be watching them from the branch right above the hammock. Zoe felt her heart leap into her throat. "It's the raven again!"

Mia sprang out of the hammock and peered up into the tree. Then she turned to face Zoe, a huge smile on her face.

"Why are you *smiling*?" Zoe asked with wide eyes.

"Because that's a crow." Mia giggled. She fell back into the hammock, and she and Zoe dissolved into a fit of relieved laughter.

Zoe couldn't seem to stop laughing. It was a good feeling after all the crazy things that had happened. As she wiped the tears of laughter from her eyes, she quickly glanced at the new pendant around her neck. Zoe held the charm in her palm and vowed silently that she would never take laughter — or good luck — for granted again.

BITE INTO THE NEXT POISON APPLE,
IF YOU DARE. . . .

Abby threw up her hands. "Unbelievable. First the lunch box." She waved her tin treasure in the air. "Then the skirt, and now *this*. We are talking serious pay dirt here. I mean, this day could go down in thrift history!"

While Lena clutched the camera and fidgeted nervously, Abby darted into another room of the old house-turned-store and emerged with the fashionable finds she had stashed in a corner. Trailing neckties, she ambled across the room and plunked everything down on a large rolltop desk. A gray-haired woman wearing a housecoat looked up from a tattered novel.

"We're ready to check out," Abby said cheerfully.

The woman didn't return her smile, and didn't speak. She simply nodded wearily, picked up a pencil, and switched on the register.

"You first." Abby nudged Lena forward. "You've been waiting a long time for this."

Lena stumbled up to the desk and reached up to remove the camera strap from around her neck. The camera felt heavier now, and though she placed the Impulse on the desk, she didn't let go right away. When she did, she realized that her palms were sweating. She felt as if she were getting a tooth filled or waiting for a shot in the doctor's office.

Probably just excitement, she told herself. Was this what it felt like to win the lottery? *Maybe it's adrenaline. Or shock.* Finding the camera certainly seemed too good to be true. . . .

"Where'd you get this?" the woman at the

register spoke for the first time, and Lena flinched, wishing she hadn't. Her voice was loud and harsh. She squinted at Lena and gave the camera a poke with her pen like it was some sort of poisonous insect.

Lena felt her excitement begin to slip away. "I . . . I . . ." she stammered, feeling foolish. She took a step back, bumping into Abby.

Abby's arm collided with the pile of loot on the desk, and half of it slid to the floor.

The woman ignored the fallen items. "Where did you get it?" she screeched. Her steely eyes were narrowed behind her reading glasses and aimed, laserlike, right at Lena.

Lena pointed toward the shelf in the back room where the Impulse had been waiting. "Right over there," she replied. She looked nervously from the back room to the camera, and then to the front door. She felt sick. She desperately wanted the camera. What if she didn't get it?

The woman's sharp gaze rested on the camera for several long moments. Then, out of the blue, her face softened. She looked almost . . . sad. But in a flash, her expression changed again. A gnarled hand reached out with alarming speed. "Well, it's not for sale!" she growled, snatching the camera and shoving it under the desk.

Lena felt as though she'd gotten the wind knocked out of her. Finding the Impulse really *was* too good to be true! She wanted to protest, but couldn't. Her bubble had burst. She couldn't speak. Or move. Or do anything. She might have just stood there deflating for the rest of the day if Abby hadn't piped up behind her.

As usual, Lena's best friend had her back . . . and (in this case) a boatload of potential purchases. "It was *on* the shelf," the bolder girl pointed out.

"Well, that was a mistake," the woman snapped. She obviously didn't appreciate being questioned.

Abby didn't flinch. "Well, I guess these are mistakes, too," she replied calmly. With a flourish she whisked the 50s dress, huge square-dance crinoline, suspenders, Boy Scout uniform, 'NSYNC lunch box, five ties, and the stack of CDs she had amassed off the rolltop and set them on a rickety table nearby. Half a second later she was arranging the dress on a hanger, prepping it to go back on the rack.

Lena almost smiled. The girl was unflappable. Abby had no intention of leaving her finds behind, Lena knew. And if her stomach wasn't still in a knot she might have enjoyed the showdown. After all, it appeared to be a pretty even match. The old woman looked fierce, but Abby was a contender.

The woman's steely eyes followed Abby as she started to walk the merchandise back to where she'd found it. Then, with a heavy sigh, she looked around the crowded, dusty shop. Shaking her head with resignation, she reached back into the desk for the camera.

"You really want this old thing?" she asked. She caught Lena's eye, and held her gaze. Her voice was gentler now, and Lena noticed laugh lines around her eyes. Maybe the old bat wasn't always this cranky. Maybe she was just having a bad day.

"Yes, I really do," Lena replied with an emphatic nod.

"Well, all right," the old woman breathed. "I'll let you have it for five dollars. Maybe it'll be good to be rid of it."

The woman smoothed a few wild gray hairs toward the knot at the back of her head while Lena dug into her pocket and swallowed a victory cry.

Five dollars! I guess I'm stealing after all! She handed over a five-dollar bill and bit back a secret smile. She would have gladly emptied her whole wallet for the camera if she had to. But she knew it was never good to let the seller see how much you want something. She should simply consider the five-dollar price tag a bonus and keep her excitement to herself.

The moment the bill left Lena's fingers she grabbed the camera and slipped the strap back around her neck. She let the Impulse rest against her side. The weight, though nothing like her digital camera, was at once familiar and comforting. She breathed a sigh of relief. It was hers. The Impulse was finally hers!

Exhilarated, the girls emerged from the dim shop into the early autumn sun. Lena's dad was leaning against the hood of the family station wagon, waiting patiently. When he saw the big bags of stuff they were carrying, he shook his head and scuffed through the thin layer of fallen leaves to open the car door.

"Your parents are never going to let me take you with me again," he told Abby, laughing as he bent over to make room in the backseat.

"Breathe easy, Mr. G.," Abby replied, giving him

a reassuring pat on the back. "My parents are familiar with my thrifting, er, problem — they won't blame you."

Lena hoped not. It would be a total bummer if Abby couldn't come treasure hunting every end of summer. Their weekend farm-town visits during peach, berry, and apple season were September highlights. And Phelps, the town they were in now, was Lena's personal favorite. The funky farm village just outside the larger city of Narrowsburg, where they all lived, was known for its antiques and luscious fruit.

Lena felt a chill as she climbed into the car, which surprised her. She'd been sweltering all day. But now, standing in the shade, she was practically shivering. She wished she'd brought a sweater.

Abby folded herself into the car behind Lena, her face aglow. Lena tried to ignore the shivers so she could bask in the celebratory mood that emanated from her friend. Even though Abby hadn't been able to talk the store owner into throwing in the ties for free, Lena could tell that she was feeling victorious. Considering that half the backseat was covered in new treasures and she was only out eighteen bucks, she should.

Abby was a professional thrifter. Both girls had been honing their skills for three years, and now, at age twelve, they were experts at finding bargains and negotiating deals. But Abby took it to the next level. She could sniff out a good find like a hound dog, and was a fierce negotiator when it came to price.

How funny that it all started by accident, Lena mused as she sat back and tried to absorb the warmth of the sunshine streaming through the window. They'd been having one of many playdates at Lena's house when Mr. Giff announced that the strawberries were ripe and he had to go to Phelps for a couple of flats. (Mr. Giff was a jam-making nut who would drive through four states for a good berry or the last peaches of the season.) Back then the girls were too young to stay home alone, so they had no choice but to go along. They'd complained loudly, but the trip turned out to be a total blast. They loaded up on berries, then hit Mr. Giff's favorite thrift store, where they found a whole collection of old Barbie dolls for practically nothing. That was all it took to get them hooked on bargain hunting.

Now the trio picked the country towns clean at the end of each summer. And this year — including today's trip — was no exception.

"I've got all my flats tucked in safe and sound," Mr. Giff announced from the front seat. "You girls get everything loaded up?"

"Sure did, Mr. G.," Abby replied as she closed the door. "We're ready to roll."

As the car pulled out of the little parking lot, Lena stared out the window, her hands folded on top of the camera. She was still thrilled to have it, but could not deny the cold whisper of worry that had descended upon her. The old lady's reaction to selling the camera had definitely been severe. Lena wondered again what had prompted her to get so . . . angry. And what had made her sell her the camera after all? Did she need the money? Business must be slow in sleepy Phelps. But then why would she sell the camera for so little?

Never mind, Lena told herself. *The important thing is that the camera is mine!* She forcefully steered her thoughts out of the shadows toward happier things — like all the fabulous stuff she was going to photograph with her new camera — and watched the familiar trees and fields flash past outside her window.

Beside her, Abby inspected her loot. "Check this out," she said, pointing to the tag on the square-dancing skirt. "Josie-Do's, get it? Like do-si-do?" The skirt had so many layers Abby was practically hidden behind it. She had to smash it down to look at the rest of her bargains.

"So, what do you think I should put in my lunch box?" she asked, running her slender fingers over Justin Timberlake's face. "My nail polish collection?"

"You could use it for, you know . . . lunch," Lena suggested.

"Brilliant!" Abby sang. "See? That is precisely why you are my best friend — nonstop great ideas."

Lena smiled distractedly and turned back toward the window just in time to see a large U-Pick strawberry patch that was closed for the season. Long, mounded rows ran from the side of the road toward the horizon, surrounded on three sides by huge wild rose hedges. It looked just like a dozen other berry fields Lena had seen in the area — nothing special.

But before she even knew what was happening Lena had raised her new camera to her eye.

What am I doing? Lena wondered. Aside from the long shadows cast by the hedges, the field was fairly flat and featureless. Kind of lonely looking, really, filled with withered berry plants and a boarded-up stand. There was no stark contrast to capture, no strong figure, no story in the frame. And yet she couldn't seem to stop herself. She felt like the camera was tugging at her finger, pulling it until . . .

She pushed the button. And to her total surprise the Impulse whirred and a piece of film emerged from the slot in the front.

"Hey, I thought there wasn't anything in there!" Abby said, looking up and leaning over to peer at the vintage contraption.

"There wasn't!" Lena exclaimed. She pulled the undeveloped picture out of the slot and turned the camera around. Sliding the button to release the little door, she looked inside. Sure enough, the battery/film compartment was still empty — no used cartridge, nothing. "This is so weird. It doesn't have film!" She shook her head, baffled, and handed the camera to Abby for additional inspection, leaning sideways so she wouldn't have to take off the strap.

"Maybe there was one last exposure jammed in the works," her dad suggested, glancing at the girls in the rearview mirror.

"Maybe . . ." Lena mumbled. She squinted at the shot. "But I doubt it'll turn out. I mean, the film has to be expired. And it wasn't even in a cartridge." Not to mention the fact that she took the picture out the window of a moving car. Blur city.

Still, Lena studied the grayish square to see if anything would show up.

Abby bent closer so she could watch, too. Neither of them breathed as out of the black, shades of blue, and then green began to emerge. Lena watched as forest-colored leaves appeared, then roses, and . . . something else.

Lena blinked, trying to figure out what it was. "Did you guys notice a water tower in that field?" she asked.

"Sorry, sweetie, I wasn't really paying attention," her dad apologized.

"Missed it." Abby shrugged.

Lena stared at the water tower growing clearer in the photo. It was one of the old-fashioned kinds, all metal, with four long, sturdy legs that looked like triangular ladders and a round tank for the water on top. The name of the town, PHELPS, was painted in giant red letters across the front of the tank. In the picture it stood in the center of the field. But in real life . . .

"I swear that wasn't there when we went by," Lena said, baffled. "It was just rows of plants, the hedge, and a boarded-up shack where the berries were sold." She could hear her voice rising along with the goose bumps popping up on her arms. Now she was *really* chilled.

Abby looked at Lena with concern. "I believe you; I just wasn't looking," she said.

Lena's dad was busy tuning in to something on the car radio and tuning out what was going on in the backseat.

"Dad, go back," Lena pleaded, leaning toward the front seat. "Please? I have to see if that tower was there."

"Wish I could, but we're already late," her dad replied. "I told your mom we'd be back by 5:30 for dinner. Maybe you just didn't see it." He shrugged. "Or maybe it's some sort of double exposure."

Lena flopped back against the backseat and looked again at the tower standing in the center of her instant picture. It hadn't been there. She was sure of it.

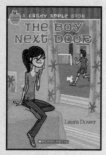